THE KELLYS OF KELVINGROVE

MARGARET THOMSON
DAVIS

THE KELLYS OF KELVINGROVE

B & W PUBLISHING

First published 2010
This edition first published 2011
by Black & White Publishing Ltd
29 Ocean Drive, Edinburgh EH6 6JL

1 3 5 7 9 10 8 6 4 2   11 12 13 14

ISBN: 978 1 84502 339 3

A CIP catalogue record for this book is available from
the British Library.

Typeset by Ellipsis Digital Limited, Glasgow
Printed and bound by CPI Cox & Wyman, Reading

ACKNOWLEDGEMENTS

Many thanks to my dear friend, Michael Malone, who wrote all the poetry in this novel.

Also my thanks to retired Detective Inspector Robert Barrowman QPN, who has conscientiously helped me with several novels.

DEDICATION

I dedicate *The Kellys of Kelvingrove* to the memory of Joe Fisher who, over many years, never failed to find answers to my research questions when he worked in the Mitchell Library.

He advised an endless number of writers who will never forget him and will always be grateful for his generous help.

I

Police officer Jack Kelly and his friend Eric Gilroy were off duty and looking forward to the Old Firm match. They were both well wrapped up in coats and woolen scarves because it was a grey, misty day.

As they met up after leaving their tenement flats, Eric said, 'We'll be lucky if we can see the match if this gets any worse.'

'It'll take more than a smir of rain and a bit of mist to stop the Old Firm match.'

Already enormous crowds were flooding the streets. Thousands of men were aiming in the same direction – Ibrox Park and the Old Firm match between Celtic and Rangers. Both Jack and Eric were wearing Rangers scarves. The nearest subway station to Ibrox was Copeland Road and the platform there was difficult to negotiate because of the mountains of mail bags lying around as a result of the postal strike. There were mail bags piled up in all sorts of places all over the town.

At last Jack and Eric were inside the stadium and standing tightly packed together with the rest of the eighty thousand spectators. A fantastic, exciting match got going. Jack and Eric clutched their heads and bawled out when Jimmy Johnstone put Celtic ahead. Then, with only seconds remaining, Colin Stein grabbed the equaliser. Bobby Lennox smashed a drive at the Rangers goal. Gerry Neef, making his first league appearance of the season for the Light Blues, touched the ball on to the bar. The ball went crashing back into play and wee Jimmy Johnstone brought out a tremendous roar from Celtic fans as he sent the ball speeding into the back of the net. That looked like the end for Rangers but up they came with a glorious Colin Stein equaliser with only seconds remaining.

Most of the spectators filed happily away towards home but at the end of the stadium where Jack and Eric were standing, something terrible started happening. People had begun to go down the stairs to leave when they thought Rangers had lost, but when the goal was scored at the last minute and there was a roar from the other fans, they turned to rush up again. This coincided with a massive number of spectators still making their way towards the exit and the subway.

Then someone carrying a young boy on his shoulders fell. Others tripped and fell on top of him. Crash barriers on the stairway were broken by the crowds as fans piled on top of one another.

Up until then, the match had been a fairly good-natured occasion with no trouble either on the terraces or on the pitch. Now, as Jack and Eric looked in horror at the twisted bodies, they were reminded of Belsen because the bodies were entangled as they had been in the pictures which came out of the concentration camps. Both Jack and Eric struggled in among the victims in a desperate effort to pull people free. Jack groaned in agony as his hip was crushed. But he used every last vestige of strength to continue to clamber around the mangle of bodies and stricken souls to save whoever he could.

Everyone, whether Rangers of Celtic supporters, forgot their normal allegiances and fought to save whoever they could in a frenzy of activity. Others were grappling onto whatever they could find to avoid falling into the carnage. One man managed to push his son over the fence to safety before he was immediately swept away with the force of the crowd. As his son shouted to him, he saw his father die upright, the life squeezed out of him.

Bodies were turning black. Others who had any breath left in them were receiving frantic help. A priest was fighting to resuscitate a man wearing Rangers colours. An Orangeman was struggling desperately to pull a Celtic supporter free.

Jack lost sight of Eric and prayed that he had escaped injury. Many people, still wearing their club colours, were trying to pull people free. Ambulances and police cars and fire engines had arrived but had some difficulty in reaching the scene because home-going crowds leaving the match, many of them drunk, were unaware of the tragedy.

Jack knew many of the police officers and one of them pulled him out.

'For God's sake, Jack, you've done enough. Go home.' Then he saw Jack limping.

'No, get into the ambulance. I'll get them to take you to the Southern General.'

'I've got to find Eric. Eric Gilroy. He was with me.'

'We'll find him, Jack. Get into the ambulance.'

'No, I'm OK. Just got a bit crushed. Isn't this a terrible tragedy? It all happened so quickly. I've never seen anything like it, have you? Come on, we'd better help to lay out the bodies.'

There were bodies in the dressing rooms, in the gymnasium, even in the laundry room. Many were already dead. Others were having resuscitation given to them by training staff. Doctors and nurses flocked to join them in doing everything possible to bring breath back to crushed bodies.

'I'll never forget,' Jack said later, 'seeing Bob Rooney, the Celtic physiotherapist, with tears in his eyes, giving the kiss of life to innumerable victims.'

Eventually Eric Gilroy was found among the dead and Jack was reduced to tears.

'He was a good, conscientious police officer.'

One of the other policemen said, 'And he died as he lived – trying to help others.'

Jack limped sadly away, knowing he would never forget this misty day of the second of January 1971.

2

Jack was persuaded to get a medical check-up. It was decided eventually that there was nothing much more they could do for his crushed hip, except he would, from now on, be confined to working limited hours in the police station and at the desk. He missed getting out and around on the beat but knew he was lucky to have survived the Ibrox tragedy and so he accepted his lot.

But he'd gone off the area where he lived. He'd gone off his tiny one-bedroomed tenement flat. It hadn't even a bathroom, just a pokey wee lavatory.

All right, he'd taken the flat originally because he had a thing – a horror in fact – of getting into debt. He had a savings account and everything he ever bought or had was paid in cash. The flat had a very low rent and that's why he and his wife Mae had moved in there. Every stick of furniture in the flat had been bought with cash. No way would he ever consider hire purchase. For one thing, he'd seen too many people get over their heads in debt and become dishonest as a result, and indeed end up in jail.

So he and his wife Mae had always lived very frugally and carefully, although he always felt a bit embarrassed, ashamed even, that he couldn't invite his friends to the flat for a meal and a bit of friendly hospitality. The kitchen in the flat was small and overcrowded with just a table and chairs and a cooker and a stand for the pots and pans. There was one other room where he and Mae slept.

They desperately needed a bigger house but it would have to be rented. A fair-sized rented house wasn't easy to come by these days. Not that Mae ever complained. She was a good-natured soul – a plump wee blonde who hardly reached past his elbow.

Indeed, she seemed perfectly happy in the tiny tenement flat. He had to sigh and shake his head at her when she said, 'As long as you're there, it's fine with me.'

Never before had it been less than fine for him. He supposed his feelings stemmed from the Ibrox disaster. He had never bothered all that much about the flat before.

But now, although he never confessed to anyone, he still had nightmares about the event. Even when he looked out the tenement window, he could see the crowds milling along towards the subway. In his nightmares, he could still see the piles of mangled corpses, some a ghastly dark blue colour, some black. Many standing up had had the life crushed out of them and had turned black.

Some people, indeed many people, had to undergo long treatments by psychiatrists after their experiences at Ibrox but he could not succumb to anything like that. He was after all a serving police officer. It was his duty, he believed, always to show courage. It was a strain, especially when he suffered continuous pain with his hip, as well as the emotional and mental strain. But he was determined to manage.

He told his pals on the beat, 'Keep your eye open for a rented place for me in a nice district, as far from my present dump as possible. OK?'

'Sure, Jack,' they all agreed. 'No problem.' Eventually, God bless them, they found a perfect place.

'How can I ever thank you,' he gasped when he saw the house and the lovely situation it was in.

'You can invite us all for slap up dinners in your posh new dining room,' they all told him.

'Don't worry,' he promised. 'I certainly will.'

3

First there were the funerals. Everyone paid their respects but what could anyone say? What consolation could anyone offer? Normally a funeral is of somebody of a ripe old age and an occasion to be treated as a celebration of that person's life. But here there had been five young lads between only thirteen and fifteen years of age from the same village. There had been lads from other places aged thirteen, fourteen, sixteen and eighteen. The oldest man, as far as Jack knew, had been in his forties.

Lord Provost Sir Donald Liddle wept at a press conference when he made an announcement about the dead.

There had been an eighteen-year-old girl who should have had the rest of her life in front of her. Apparently, she had been a great Rangers supporter and she had made a wee doll of Colin Stein. She worked in a factory and the girls who worked beside her dared her to go to Ibrox and deliver it to him personally. And because she was a cheery extrovert of a girl, she did.

Jack found the funeral services nearly reduced him to tears each time. He imagined how the families of the victims must be feeling. He admired the football players of both teams who turned up each time to pay their respects. Police officers attended as well.

Jack said to one of them, 'The worst of all is they were so young. They should have been able to enjoy so many more years of life.'

'I know, and there's nothing that any of us can say to the families that would be of any help or comfort.'

It seemed to go on endlessly and only the thought of the house his police officer pals had found for him kept Jack going. Over and over, he imagined welcoming them into the spacious dining room and treating them to a good dinner. It would be his way of thanking them for literally saving his bacon. There had been so many times recently when he thought he was going mad.

He hadn't discussed the house with Mae yet. The Ibrox tragedy and the attention to the families took obvious precedence over everything else. Mae was friendly with Eric Gilroy's wife who was broken-hearted at losing Eric and so all Mae's attention and most of her time went to her friend.

On his way home from one of the funerals, Jack had gone with one of his police officer friends to have another look at the house.

'God, Charlie. I can hardly believe my luck with it being so near the Kelvingrove Art Galleries as well.'

'Yeah, that's a really beautiful building, isn't it?' Charlie said. 'And look up there. You wouldn't even need to walk all round the park to get there.'

Jack gazed across the narrow part of the Kelvin River to where, past a line of trees further on, there was a very rough, very steep slope. At the top was an area at the back of the Galleries where there was a car park and a large fountain.

He laughed. 'If I felt nimble enough. But I can't see me making a climb like that with my hip. Not to worry though, it won't take long going round the park way to either the front or the back of the Galleries.'

'It's damnable that Eric won't be here to see you move into

your house, Jack. Or to come and have the slap up feeds you've promised us.'

'I know. As somebody said, he died as he lived – a good police officer trying his best to help people. We'll drink to his memory, Charlie.'

'Yeah, definitely. He won't be forgotten. Talking of drinks, how about us going round to the Art Galleries restaurant now and having a bite to eat and a drink.'

'Good idea.'

They tried to keep cheerful as they walked but the aura of the funerals they had both been attending still clung around them. Once in the restaurant, however, they felt slightly better. The area they settled into was fronted with glass that looked out on to an interesting view of the outside of the Galleries. They tried their best to relax and shake off the memories that depressed them so much.

After a couple of drinks, Charlie said, 'It's not surprising we're feeling so low, Jack. I mean, to be so closely involved in such a tragedy, and then all the funerals.'

'And the tragedy of the families. I'm haunted by their obvious grief, Charlie. I confess I still see their faces in bed at night. It puts me off my sleep just thinking about them.'

'Have you tried a stiff whisky before you go to bed?'

'Good idea.'

'That's what helps me.'

'You feel the same then?'

'Of course I do. We all do. We'd be inhuman not to be seriously affected by it. Let's order another whisky now and on your way home, you can buy a bottle and start taking that bedtime drink.'

'Don't worry. I will.'

Although he doubted if even downing the whole bottle would cure how bad he felt.

4

'But darling, I don't want to move,' Mae Kelly said. 'It's so convenient for the shops and everything.'

Jack groaned. 'Don't be ridiculous, Mae. It's practically prehistoric. One room and kitchen and lavatory. Not even a bathroom. The house I've got the chance of has three bedrooms, a sitting room, a big dining room and a bathroom. And it's in a beautiful situation. What could be better? At least come with me to see it.'

She certainly didn't feel a hundred per cent happy about the move but where her handsome police officer husband went, she would go to. She adored the black-haired, cleft-chinned, dark-eyed Jack. She felt sorry for him too. He had been injured in the Ibrox disaster and was left with a painful limp. As a result, he worked permanent day shift behind the front desk of the local police station.

'We've been very lucky to get the chance of this Waterside Way house, especially with it being rented. On my wages, we'd never have enough cash to buy any property, but with all our savings over the years, we can just afford to rent.'

Mae hesitated. 'You could get a mortgage, Jack.'

'Now, Mae, you know how I feel about owing money.'

She did indeed. Jack always insisted that he'd never owed

11

a penny in his life and never would. She admired him enormously for his strong principles. There were few people who had any principles at all these days. They lived very frugally but as a result, they each were even able to keep a savings account going.

She loved so many things about Jack, including his love making. He was so sexually passionate. And Jack was always right. As a result, she went along with him to look at the Waterside Way house. It was the first house in a row of seven houses, all joined together, each with a garage attached. There was a sitting room and a dining room and a kitchen downstairs and upstairs was a bathroom and three bedrooms. At the end of Waterside Way there was a path with a small wooden footbridge over a narrow part of the River Kelvin. At the other side of the river was a line of trees and a rough, steep slope stretching up beyond the trees. Eventually, in the distance, the back of the imposing Kelvingrove Art Galleries could be seen.

'What do you think?' Jack asked.

'Oh, it's lovely,' Mae said.

'You'd better have a look out the back.'

There was a muddy slope at the back of the houses, then the slope reached down to the quiet Museum Road. Beyond was park land and then the University of Glasgow and the Hunterian Museum.

'Actually, it's got the best of both worlds,' Jack said. 'Like being in the country, yet near to town. So we'll take it. OK?'

'Yes, of course.'

Her heart warmed with love towards Jack. Trust him to get something wonderful like this. Probably he'd asked all the police officers on the beat to keep an eye open for somewhere nice. Anyway, now that she'd seen the place, she was happy and looking forward to the move. She could hardly wait. It was then, unexpectedly, that the trouble started.

Jack had said he was looking forward to sleeping in a 'proper bed'. Not a hole-in-the-wall bed, as the one in the tenement flat was called. So was she, but it hadn't occurred to her what a 'proper bed' would cost. Then there was the paint and wallpaper needed. Not to mention new carpets and furniture for the extra bedrooms. It obviously hadn't occurred to Jack either. And she hadn't the heart to worry him. She even got into the habit of quoting prices less than what she paid.

He said she couldn't hang up her rusty-looking utensils in their lovely, newly-painted kitchen and so she'd even had to buy new kitchen equipment. In no time, their small savings account was empty and she had to order all the big stuff like furniture and carpets from a wholesale warehouse. She imagined that in the two or three months that the warehouse might take to send in their account, she would have saved up enough again to cover it.

Jack loved the new house and was so proud of it.

But then the warehouse account came in and she nearly died of shock. She had never been faced with such a huge bill in her life. She felt so dazed by it that she could hardly pay any attention to a very posh neighbour, a Mrs Charlotte Arlington-Jones from house number five – a tall woman with a long nose. She had come to tell her of the 'ghastly neighbours in number three and four' and how they should all get together and complain to the authorities until the 'ghastly creatures' were removed. Apparently number three housed the Shafaatullas, a Pakistani Muslim family. Two gay men lived in number four.

Letters about the warehouse bill began arriving, threatening court proceedings and all sorts of awful things if the account was not paid immediately. Mae became distraught. She wandered about in a daze. She didn't know how she managed to carry on with her normal housework. She even attended a meeting organised by Mrs Arlington-Jones from house number

13

five. Others at the meeting were Mrs Jean Gardner from number six – another posh lady but with a kind face and gentle voice. She was immaculately turned out with dark hair piled on top of her head and face carefully made up and long artificial nails painted deep red. There was also Doris McIvor and her mother from house number two, Mae's next door neighbour. Elderly Mrs McIvor was obviously suffering from serious dementia. The man from number seven was a tall skeleton of man with wild-looking eyes. He was called the Reverend Denby and was a retired minister from the Highlands.

The meeting took place in Mrs Arlington-Jones's sitting room – a curious group of neighbours chatting in a desultory manner while Mrs Arlington-Jones bustled about.

'Right, ladies and gentlemen, I've called this meeting to complain about the new tenants in our exclusive little enclave here. I believe that it will lower the tone of the place with that large family of Asian people moving in here. I shudder to think how many of them there are. And I dread to think what they'll be getting up to. Everyone knows they have ghastly bad taste. They are likely to paint the outside of that house a bright pink or purple or something – and as for that awful smell of curry! Well, what more can I say?'

She sat back and folded her arms, waiting for a response from the others. Quite a lively debate ensued.

Mae Kelly and Doris McIvor worriedly said, 'Now, we don't really know that they'll be in any way offensive, do we?'

Mrs Jean Gardner said gently, 'They come from the Gorbals, dear, and we all know what a rough place that is. I wish them no harm, of course, but I do believe they won't be happy here, being so out of place. It's just not right for them.'

The Reverend Denby called things to order rather tetchily.

'But what about the poofs? Surely someone else noticed them.'

'I think you'll find their house immaculate and if I may

say so, in rather good taste,' Mrs Gardner said in her quiet, gentle tone. 'They are both teachers, you know. And artists. Mr Clive Westley is an art teacher in a private school.'

'They are wicked, dirty poofs. They get up to disgusting perversions behind their closed door. They are worse than those non-believers you're on about.'

After more arguing and deliberation, it was decided that they should protest discreetly about all of the new tenants.

Doris gave in because her mother was beginning to misbehave and repeat everything endlessly to everyone's annoyance.

Mae's mind was so desperately worried about her own business that she just agreed for peace. She even agreed to Mrs Gardner's suggestion that she should ask Jack to write a letter to the Council because, being a police officer, his letter would be taken notice of more than a letter from any of the other tenants.

The meeting closed on that 'satisfactory note'. She kept her promise and said to Jack, 'There's been a meeting and the woman in number five wants you to write a letter to the Council asking them to get rid of the Pakistanis in number three and the two gay men in number four. Mrs Arlington-Jones says, and I quote her, "They are totally unsuitable and unacceptable."'

Jack flicked her an impatient glance from over the top of his newspaper.

'Tell them to go to hell. The Pakistanis and the gay blokes haven't broken any laws.'

She tried to keep an active mind, filling it with garbled prayers about somehow being able to pay the warehouse bill. She tried to keep her body active as well. She scrubbed floors all over the house, over and over again, as if by keeping so wildly and frantically active, she could scrub her terror away.

Then, as if by some miracle, her prayers were answered. As she madly thrashed about with a scrubbing brush in the hall cupboard, a splinter of wood shot up under her finger-nail, driven by her frantic scrubbing. Eyes watering with the pain, she furiously battered at the split wood on the floor to relieve her anger and pain. It was then she noticed she had loosened one of the floorboards. She thought she caught a glimpse of something coloured through the crack. After sucking her finger free of its hurt, she gingerly lifted the loose board.

She would never forget her astonishment at what she saw underneath. There were several neat bundles of used £5 notes. Hysterical gasps of joy careered around the cupboard in which she was kneeling. God had answered her prayers after all. She snatched the piles of notes and stuffed them into her apron pockets. She got up and gave a wild dance of delight.

Then gradually, caution crept over her. She mustn't tell Jack, or anyone else, about her find. Not yet. Not until she'd paid her warehouse bill and then saved up and conscientiously put back every penny she'd taken. Then she could tell Jack, as if she'd just newly discovered the money. The police could then make the necessary enquiries as to how it got there and who it had originally belonged to.

Probably it was the previous tenant of the house who had died, some old miser perhaps, or an eccentric who didn't trust banks. She'd heard of people like that.

Replacing the board, she struggled to her feet. She would pay the warehouse bill immediately. Her terrible problem was solved, that was the main thing. She felt joyously, hysterically relieved and happy.

And yet . . . Not only caution but a strange uneasiness darted about like mice in the darkest corners of her mind.

With a hasty, furtive gesture, she shut the cupboard door. And as she did so, her hand trembled. Somehow she felt she had far more reason to be afraid now than she ever had before.

5

Mrs Jean Gardner from number six had begun to visit Doris and Mrs McIvor at number two nearly every day. She spoke gently to Doris, telling her not to worry. She'd help her get to the root of the problem and everything would be all right.

'Do you think, dear, you could have done something?' she asked with a worried expression. 'You might have, quite unintentionally of course, done something to the poor helpless old lady to have caused her to withdraw from the world. Probably she imagines she'd doing it for her own safety, dear.' Mrs Gardner added, 'Do you think she's even afraid of you?'

'Oh no,' Doris protested. 'There could be no need for her to feel afraid of me. I'd never do her any harm. She knows that. I've always been as kind as I could to her.'

Mrs Gardner placed a soft white hand on Doris's knee, her long scarlet nails shimmering in the light from the standard lamp.

'Now, my dear.' Her voice was so gentle, it was almost a whisper. 'Look into your heart and remember I care about you and am trying to help you in any way I can. But try to search in the deepest, darkest corners of your mind. Ask yourself if you've ever been impatient or angry with the poor helpless old lady. Have you never been tempted to lash out at her?'

Doris felt herself begin to tremble with distress. Haltingly she admitted, 'I suppose there have been times when I've been so frightened and upset by some of the things Mother does – like running out of the house. It's just . . . It's just that I'm afraid she'll come to some harm.'

'But my dear, *why* does the poor helpless old lady run away from you?'

'She's . . . she's ill. She doesn't know what she's doing. But she keeps doing things and I can't help getting impatient and upset and . . . And . . .'

'Harm her?'

'No, no, I'd never harm my mother. She was so good to me when I was growing up. I'll never forget that.'

'My dear.' Mrs Gardner's voice became quietly accusing. 'I saw you yesterday grab her roughly by the arm and drag her back into the house. You jerked her off her feet. I heard her cry out in pain. That's why I've been so worried and want to help you.'

Tears gushed up to Doris's eyes. 'But I'd got such a fright. I'd gone to the bathroom and when I came back out, she'd disappeared from the sitting room, where I thought she'd dozed off to sleep in the arm chair. I was afraid she might fall into the river. I found her quite near the river. She could have fallen in.'

'There's a little footbridge, dear. She was trying to reach the little footbridge and escape from you. I hear her saying that, or words to that effect.'

Doris was weeping helplessly now.

'I didn't mean to hurt her.'

Mrs Gardner sighed. 'So you did harm her?'

'No, I mean . . . I grabbed her arm but I didn't mean to hurt her.'

Mrs Gardner patted Doris's hand. 'Try to calm yourself, dear, and forgive yourself. I'll come back tomorrow to help you. We'll work this out between us, don't worry. I know you're a good daughter. We just must find a way to calm you down.'

Doris, still weeping, saw her neighbour to the outside door and watched the elegant, beautifully dressed figure with glossy dark hair and little pearl earrings and designer suit walk along Waterside Way. Only when she had disappeared into the garden, then the house at number six did Doris retreat back into her own house.

She ached to speak to Mrs Gardner again to try and convince her that she had never done her mother any harm. What she secretly agonised about, of course, was that there had been times recently when she felt like throttling her mother. She prayed Mrs Gardner would save her from herself and save her mother. Guilt about her violent feelings had begun eating into her very soul. Her mother had been so good to her when she was little and while she was growing up. Her loving kindness could not be denied and Doris didn't want to deny it. But her mother now was like a different person. It wasn't only that she kept disappearing, often in the middle of the night, but she kept repeating everything. She kept asking the same questions over and over and over again. Doris feared it was driving her mad.

Mrs Gardner had been able to read her innermost secret mind, the part of her mind that wanted – dare she admit even to herself – to kill her mother.

Mrs Gardner was a beautiful kindly woman who would do her best to help her and prevent her from doing anything dreadful. She ached for Mrs Gardner to come back and help her. She ached for anyone to help her.

She truly loved her mother and was desperately afraid of doing her any harm.

6

Mae was trying her best to save enough five pound notes to replace the money she'd stolen. She needed tights and new pants, to mention just a couple of things, but she denied herself them and everything else. In the middle of all this worry, it didn't help when Mrs Jean Gardner, the neighbour from number six, began coming in. First she'd go into Doris and Mrs McIvor's house next door and then she'd come knocking at her door. Mae didn't like her, couldn't take to her, even imagined there was something suspicious about her. Of course, it could just be, Mae secretly admitted, that she was too worried about the awful things she herself had done and was just transferring her own guilt on to this very caring, kind and perfectly innocent woman.

'Are you all right, dear?' Mrs Gardner asked gently once they'd settled into the black leather easy chairs in the sitting room.

'Yes, why shouldn't I be all right?' Immediately the words were out Mae felt ashamed of their sharp tone. 'I'm sorry,' she added. 'I'm feeling a bit stressed just now.'

'Well, I don't blame you, my dear,' Mrs Gardner stretched over a soft white hand and patted Mae's knee, 'with the worry you have to contend with just now.'

Mae suddenly felt faint. Did this woman actually know about the theft of the five-pound notes? But how could she?

'I . . . I . . .' she stammered in distress. 'I don't . . . I don't know what you mean.'

'You poor thing,' Mrs Gardner sympathised. 'It must be awful for you.'

'How do you . . . How do you know? I don't understand.'

'I saw it, dear, with my own eyes.'

'You saw it?' Mae really believed she was about to lose consciousness. 'When did you see it? How could you?'

'This morning, dear.'

'But you couldn't have.'

'Oh, but I assure you I did, dear. And of course it made me very sad.'

'But I've been in the house all morning.'

'I know, dear. I know.'

'Then how could you? I don't know what you're talking about.'

'Your husband, dear. What an unusually handsome man he is.'

'My husband?' Mae felt a wonderful wave of relief engulf her. She collapsed back into the scarlet satin cushion of the chair. She even managed a smile. 'Yes, he is handsome, isn't he? I'm very luck to have him.'

'Yes, dear, and you want to keep him, of course.'

'Of course.' Mae began to feel uneasy again. What was the woman on about now?

'So you're doing something about it, are you?'

Mae gasped with impatience. 'About what?'

Mrs Gardner patted Mae's knee again. 'The other woman, dear.'

'The other woman?' Mae couldn't help a laugh escaping. What a bloody menace Mrs Jean Gardner was. A real stirrer of trouble. Mae could believe that she was the one behind

21

Mrs Arlington-Jones calling the meeting and getting all het up about the gay men and the Pakistanis.

'If you're suggesting, Mrs Gardner, that my husband is having some sort of secret affair, I can assure you you're wrong.'

'I do admire your faith and loyalty, dear,' Mrs Gardner said gently, 'but I'm sorry to say that I saw them together.'

'My husband is a police officer. People approach him all the time for help and advice. He knows lots of women through his work.'

'I understand he only works inside the local police station, dear. He doesn't go out on the beat.'

'That's right.'

'I saw this woman get into his car outside the police station, dear. A very attractive young woman she was.'

'Mrs Gardner, the woman would have been in the station asking for help and advice. No doubt she was so upset with her problem that my husband felt it his duty to see her safely home. That's why she'd be getting into his car.'

'I do admire your faith and loyalty, dear,' Mrs Gardner repeated. She glanced at her watch. 'I'm sorry, I have to go now. I promised to pop in and see Mrs Arlington-Jones. But don't worry, dear. I'll see you again tomorrow and I'll do what I can to support and help you.'

Speechless at the cheek of the woman, Mae saw her to the door but didn't return the wave of the scarlet-nailed hand. She went back to the sitting room and collapsed into her chair.

'Well,' she said out loud, 'could you beat that? What a creep of a woman. No, a wicked woman. Wait till Jack hears about this.'

Then she thought, no, probably Jack would be furious and she had enough worry and trouble to contend with without stirring up any more.

7

The long-nosed woman was watching him – white women were very cheeky. He could never quite get used to how free they were. How they made eye contact. Mahmood was still shocked by this. It was most disconcerting. He prayed to Allah that the woman would go away.

He was examining the outside of the house. It was structurally sound but it seemed very sad and dilapidated. The last tenant, an old grandmother, had lived in it alone and could not have been expected to clean and paint it. He had met her and her family before she moved out. Or rather, before her family moved her out and put her in an institution. That was another thing about the British life he would never get used to and which shocked him most deeply. They did not care for their families.

In the whole of India and Pakistan, there would not be as many abandoned and lonely people as there were in this one Scottish city of Glasgow. In Britain, widowers and widows, grandfathers, grandmothers, unmarried uncles and aunties by the million lived separately from their relations and were lonely. They lived in dingy slum tenements like those in the Gorbals, or in nice places in the West End.

What did it matter where you were if you were lonely and abandoned and no one paid you any respect?

They had gone to pay their respects to the old grandmother who had been the previous tenant in number three. Rasheeda, the mother of his children, could not speak much English so she sat very quietly but his teenage children, Zaida and tall, handsome Mirza, spoke most politely. Bashir, his son-in-law, was at work and could not be with them. They owned a successful grocery business. It wasn't a very large shop but it had a splendid variety of groceries and newspapers too. Bashir worked hard and conscientiously in the shop since he'd lost his wife, Mahmood's dear daughter, in a gas explosion in which his parents had also died. The house had been completely destroyed, along with everything in it.

The old lady had chuckled and said, 'The neighbours are going to have kittens having you lot beside them, especially that snobby woman in number five. But good luck to you, I say, and thanks for coming to see me.'

He did not understand why the neighbours were going to have kittens but the visit had obviously pleased the old grandmother and made her happy. And so he was happy. His lean brown face stretched into a smile.

He would never understand how the old lady's son could have so cruelly given her away, instead of welcoming her into his own home. The prophet Mohammed (may Allah's peace and blessings be on him) said, 'The Lord has decreed . . . that ye show kindness to your parents. If one of them or both of them attain old age with thee, say not – fie – unto them or repulse them, but speak unto them a gracious word and lower unto them the wing of submission through mercy and say: My Lord, Have mercy on them both as they did care for me when I was little.'

He wondered if she wanted them to visit her again to keep

24

her company and pay their respects. He thought it might be cheeky of him and so he just waited for her to invite them. They hung around the bed repeating polite goodbyes but no invitation came.

His house at number three was exactly the same in layout and proportions, he understood, as the other houses. All had a sitting room, a dining room and a kitchen downstairs. Upstairs there was a bathroom and three bedrooms. Each house had a garage attached to one side.

He and Bashir had much painting to do before they moved in. Rasheeda much cleaning and polishing. But it was a good house with a garden at the front, something they thanked Allah for. Bashir used to live in a very good district with his wealthy parents far from the Gorbals and had a garden there. But Mahmood had never had a garden before. At the end of the garden was a path and a narrow stretch of the River Kelvin, then a line of trees. Beyond that was a rough slope which led to the back of the Kelvingrove Art Galleries and Museum.

Oh, many a fascinating hour he and his family would spend in that beautiful place. His small frame trembled with pleasurable anticipation. He could hardly wait. The family at present, however, were busy cleaning the old house so that it was left in a respectable condition.

Now the removal men had arrived at the back of the house in Museum Road. Mahmood rushed through the empty house to open the door, shouting and brandishing the keys. Already the removal men had the back of their van open and were punching and jerking at his furniture. In his excitement, Mahmood spoke quickly and loudly in Urdu.

'Aye, aw right, dad,' one of the men said, without looking round. 'Keep your whiskers on.'

Another man said, 'Christ, the posh yins round about here are goin' tae go a bundle on this!'

25

Mahmood flicked a worried gaze around. No sign of his family yet.

He felt naked without them. It was most strange to be on his own. And in such a strange place. It was almost as different from the Gorbals as the Gorbals had been different from his homeland. But at least the Gorbals had been noisy and had many children. Here, away from the main road and the noise of traffic, it was still and quiet. Nowhere had he ever been used to quietness.

The removal men were staggering towards the back door, chins glued to a large, old-fashioned sideboard. They were cursing because of the muddy quagmire their feet were sinking and slithering into. Mahmood squeezed back against the wall and called to them instructions about where in the dining room to put the sideboard. At the same time he kept an anxious watch on his other possessions in case any thief came by.

Next from the van appeared the bed settee. It had been covered in green cloth by his wife Rasheeda, who was very clever with the sewing machine. The bed settee was very useful as an extra bed. It would be a long time before they could afford to buy another.

Chairs were balanced on the pavement of Museum Road and a rolled-up striped mattress tied tightly with string. He slithered down to try and lift a cardboard box. It was full of pots and pans and it rattled and clanged noisily.

'Look, will ye jist leave everything to us, dad. Away ye go back into the house. Ye're like a wee bird hoppin' about out here.'

He was not insulted. Everyone Scottish was all right to him and his family. They were happy with the Scottish people.

'Excuse me. I give you much trouble.'

'Aye, ye're right, auld yin. Away ye go in and make yersel' a nice wee cup o' Pakistani tea.'

Mahmood laughed. Yet at the same time, it occurred to him that these men would not see anything funny or out of place about a man doing women's work. It was the Western way.

His son-in-law, Bashir, had obviously long since adopted Western ways. To hear Bashir talk with his Glasgow accent, no one would have guessed he was not a true Glaswegian. Only his brown face gave him away.

It was then that he heard Bashir calling from the open front door. He must have left one of his assistants to look after the shop.

'Are you there, Pop?' No one else but Bashir ever called him by this Glasgow word.

'Yes, Bashir. I am here helping the removal men.'

Staggering past Bashir, one of the removal men said, 'Will ye remove this auld yin. He's gettin' in oor way.'

'OK.' Bashir laughed. 'Come on, Pop. I'll make you a nice cup of tea.'

Mahmood tutted. He had reprimanded Bashir about this before but it had not done the slightest good. Bashir was such a kindly, good-natured man. No one could be angry with him for long.

Through in the kitchen, Bashir found the kettle and splashed it full of water.

'Nice place, eh? Where's Rasheeda?'

'They are finishing off cleaning the old house. But it is time Zaida and Mirza were home from school. I hope they have not lost their way.' He scuttled towards the front door. 'I will see if they are approaching.'

Bashir shouted after him.' The tea won't be a minute.'

Mahmood stood in the small front garden and gazed anxiously beyond the river, trying to peer between the trees at the other side, until suddenly he spied the tall figure of Mirza (such a handsome boy) and his sister, Zaida. There was also another girl with them, a white girl with a thick cap of red-gold curls. She waved goodbye and walked further along the path.

'Who was your companion?' Mahmood asked once he had hustled brother and sister into the house.

'Sandra. She lives with her mother at number five,' Mirza said. 'Her father is dead.'

'Poor girl,' Mahmood sympathised. 'We must have her and her mother here for tea, after we are properly settled in. Rasheeda will make chapattis.'

Zaida laughed. 'Sandra Arlington-Jones. Double-barrelled, no less.'

'Double-barrelled,' Mahmood repeated in puzzlement. By this time, the removal men had finished their work and Bashir was offering them a cup of tea.

'Och, we've another load to deliver and they'll be waiting for us. We'd better get on with it, but thanks aw the same, pal.'

And off they went. No sooner had their big van disappeared than Rasheeda arrived.

'You look done in, Ma. Sit down and I'll give you a cup of tea.'

Mahmood tutted and shook his head but didn't say anything. After the tea, they all had a look around their new home and felt well pleased and happy.

'Such a nice area too,' Rasheeda said. 'Like being away out in the country.'

'I can hear the river,' Zaida put a cupped hand to her ear, 'and footsteps echoing on the wee footbridge.'

Mahmood thought his children were getting very westernised. He sighed and accepted the fact. His children were getting a good education. They had a nice new home, good prospects and good Scottish friends. He should feel lucky and grateful, and happy.

And he did.

8

'It's awful kind of you to come in,' Doris McIvor said as she poured out cups of tea. 'Is it all right if I call you Mae?' Doris had a dark frizzy mop of grey-streaked hair that gave her a wild look.

'Of course.' Mae had felt worried about the bad effect Mrs Gardner might have on Doris and her mother and had decided to keep an eye on Doris and try to warn her about the awful hypocrite of a neighbour.

'I seldom get out because of Mum. I mean, I can't leave her alone and I don't always feel welcome if I take her with me.'

'I could see what you mean at the meeting. I didn't like the way Mrs Arlington-Jones treated you and your mother. But we didn't get a chance to talk then. I'd be careful about that Mrs Gardner too, Doris.'

'Oh, Mrs Gardner's all right. Almost angelic, in fact. She's been so kind to me. She visits me nearly every day.'

Mae looked worried. 'Really?'

'The meeting was embarrassing,' Doris admitted. 'Mum wasn't always like that. She was wonderful to me and my brother when we were younger and when she was in good health. I must never forget that.'

'What day is it?' Mrs McIvor suddenly asked. She had smooth white hair, pinned severely back with kirby grips.

'Tuesday, Mum.'

'I was just thinking,' Mae said, 'anytime you need to get out for a break, I don't mind coming in for an hour. As long as it's while my husband's at work.'

'Oh, thank you so much.'

Mae was taken aback to see how Doris had suddenly taken a fit of violent trembling.

'I'm so lucky having such a good neighbour. You're a lovely person, Mae Kelly.'

'Are you all right, Doris?' Mae asked anxiously.

'Your husband's a lucky man. You're lovely looking as well.'

'What? Me? I'm wee and fat.'

'You're a curvaceous blonde and I bet your hair's naturally curly.'

'Well, yes. But have you seen my husband? That's what I call good-looking.'

'What day is it?' Mrs McIvor asked.

'Tuesday, Mum,' Doris answered, obviously struggling to be patient.

'Where's your brother. Can he not help out?'

'Australia.'

'Oh dear. Anyway, I could come in for an hour each Thursday morning – say ten thirty to eleven thirty, just to let you have a wee break on your own. Even a walk around the Art Galleries and maybe a cup of tea in the café might do you good.'

'You don't know what that would mean to me, Mae. I'll never be able to thank you enough.'

'Och, don't be daft. It's nothing. Just an hour a week. I'd like to help more but I've so much to do in the house and an awful lot on my mind just now.'

'Ten thirty on Thursday morning.' Doris repeated the words as if saying a prayer.

'What day is it?'

'Tuesday, Mum.'

'You said Thursday.'

'No, Thursday is when Mae is coming to visit you. Today is Tuesday.' Then to Mae, 'She's on tranquillizers during the day and sleeping tablets at night but she nods off quite a lot during the day. I've to be so careful never to forget her tranquillizers, otherwise she'd get out of the house, even if I locked the door. It's a worry if I've to leave her even when I need to go to the bathroom.'

'I didn't get my tablets today.'

'Yes, you did, Mum.'

'You didn't give me my tablets today.'

'Yes, I did, Mum.'

'What day is it?'

'Tuesday, Mum.'

Mae detected the mounting stress in Doris's voice and posture.

'You see,' Doris went on, 'she'd be out of the house and away without somebody here to keep an eye on her.'

'I was a nurse for a while after I left school.'

'I'm not a bit surprised. You're such a capable, caring person.'

Mae could have laughed. Caring, yes, but definitely not capable. If she had been capable of managing her affairs, she would not have got herself into such a mess of debt, and now theft. And her the wife of a police officer. She felt so desperately ashamed, she could have wept.

'What day is it?'

'Tuesday, Mum. I could give her an extra tranquillizer before you come in. It wouldn't do her any harm, just make her more likely to doze off for a wee while.'

'I didn't get any tablets today.'

'Yes, you did, Mum.' The stress in Doris's voice had begun to make Mae feel nervous. It was as if Doris could explode at any minute. Her frizzy hair was practically standing up on end.

'I'd better go.'

'You see, she could be liable to wander out of the house and away without someone here to keep an eye on her.'

'What day is it?'

'Tuesday, Mum. I could give her an extra tranquillizer before you come in. It wouldn't do her any harm, just make her doze off for a wee while.'

Doris obviously didn't realise that she'd begun to repeat herself.

'I didn't get my tablets today.'

'Yes, you did, Mum.'

'What day is it?'

'Tuesday.'

Mae felt truly sorry for Doris. It was enough to drive anyone mad listening to the old woman, all day and every day.

She hesitated. 'Have you ever thought of – you know – a home?'

'Often. But my brother would be furious with me. He doesn't understand. He hasn't been over for a while and Mum was fine then – a bit forgetful, that was all. When I suggested it, he was so shocked. I thought he was never going to stop going on and on about how cruel and selfish I was.'

'Tell him to come over now and see her for himself.'

'Oh, I have. But he's got a really important and responsible job, and a young family to consider. He can't just walk away from everything at the drop of a hat or on one of my whims, he says.'

'Whims!' Mae echoed. 'I'd teach him. I'd do it anyway.'

But of course she knew she wouldn't. She'd be just as stupid as Doris was with her brother. And just as soft as Doris was with her mother.

Wasn't she being stupid and soft with Jack? She adored

him, of course, but she had been suffering hell over the warehouse account and trying to be as economical as she could in order to save up to pay it. Then there was the worse hell of worrying about how she'd save enough to pay back all she'd stolen from under the floor boards.

And all the time, Jack kept happily inviting all his police officer pals to show off his new house and to have a meal in his lovely new dining room.

Mae rose to go. 'I'll see you on Thursday.'

'You said it was Tuesday,' Mrs McIvor complained.

'Today is Tuesday, Mum. Mae is just telling me that she'll be back for another visit.'

Mae gave Doris a sympathetic hug before leaving.

Reaching her own front door, she relaxed and breathed a sigh of relief. As she did so, she noticed two scruffily dressed young men approaching towards the footbridge. Then they stopped on the bridge lighting cigarettes as soon as Jack's Mini appeared. In a couple of minutes, Jack was at the front door, grabbing her into his arms. As usual, she marvelled at his handsome appearance. He especially suited his police uniform.

'Darling.' He hugged her enthusiastically and she noticed, as she glimpsed over his shoulder, that the two men had disappeared. She had noticed them in the first place because it was so unusual to see anyone at this quiet end of the river. Everyone came from the many streets beyond the front of the Art Galleries and they walked along and into the Galleries by the front entrance. If they used the back entrance, and lots of people did, there was plenty of room for parking cars or walking about. She had never seen anyone venture beyond that wide area to scramble down the rough slope and make for the river's edge. She felt increasingly uneasy, frightened even.

Soon she was busy serving up the evening meal. As usual, it was food from Marks & Spencer. Jack insisted she always shopped there for food. It was delicious, of course, and they enjoyed it but she couldn't help saying, 'I'll have to stop doing this.'

'Doing what?' Jack asked.

'Buying so much food from Marks & Spencer. We can't afford it. After this I'm going to the nearest supermarket.'

'Oh, for God's sake, Mae.' Jack hitched up his jacket and pushed two pound notes across the table to her. 'There's a raise in your housekeeping money.'

She suddenly had an unusual and violent urge to stuff the paltry pounds down Jack's throat but just at that moment, the telephone jangled. She answered it.

'It's for you.' She held out the receiver and Jack heaved himself out of his chair. He had admitted before now that at the end of each day, he suffered agonising pain with his injured hip. His limp certainly became more obvious. It made her feel guilty that she had allowed herself to even think impatient thoughts about him.

'Harry! Of course you can join us, old son, and welcome. See you on Sunday. We can catch up with all the news then.'

That meant, she knew, that yet another steak pie or fish and chip supper had to be purchased for the Sunday police get-togethers. She was about to object but watching Jack limp back to his chair, she hadn't the heart. Her anger fizzled out. She loved the stupid, thoughtless man. That would always be the trouble. In bed at night, enfolded in his arms, experiencing him plunging deep inside her, she didn't care about anything else he did, as long as he kept making such passionate love to her.

She struggled for control.

'Had a busy day?'

'Yeah. The lads have been questioning a couple of neds about a robbery at the Art Galleries but they released them eventually.'

34

'The Art Galleries?'

'Yeah. We know it was them. It had their fingerprints all over it. As well as giving them the third degree, the lads searched their pad, but with no luck. They didn't expect any, of course.'

'A painting, was it?'

'No, cash. From the gift shop. It's always cash with them.'

Mae began to feel faint.

'So you had to let them go.'

'Meantime. But the lads aren't worried. They know they'll get them. They'll have hidden the cash somewhere and they'll not be able to wait to collect it. Soon the lads'll visit them again and nab them with it. It's happened before. They're a couple of stupid toe rags. Always have been.'

Mae had to sit down. She was remembering the two men she'd seen approaching down the slope towards the river's edge. She was remembering the cash under the floorboards.

She felt sick.

9

Clive Westley was small and delicate-looking with short, light brown hair. Paul Brownlee was tall and had longish dark brown hair. They both lived at number four. Today they were excited. Something good had happened to both of them at the same time – a most unusual occurrence. One of Clive's paintings had been accepted to be hung in the National Gallery in Edinburgh, and a book of Paul's poems had been accepted for publication. They hugged one another and showered each other with kisses. Wonderful, wonderful! Truly a gift from God. They both had been trying for years to get any sort of success with their creative work, while at the same time holding down regular jobs to make a living. Clive had painted innumerable scenes of the Scottish countryside while he and Paul were on holiday. Unexpectedly, the painting that was to be hung in the National Gallery was one he'd done of a tenement close. It had caught his eye with its coloured wall tiles and stained glass window. It was in a building near where he worked as an art teacher in a small, private, boys-only school.

Paul was also a teacher, but he taught English in a large secondary school. He'd always loved to write and had penned many poems without ever getting any published. He'd also written a couple of novels, without success. They had both been historical in context. One was set during the First World War, the other in the fifties.

Although his main ambition was to have a novel published, Paul quite enjoyed writing poetry and eventually had gathered enough poems to make a slim volume. At least writing poetry kept his creative juices flowing. To get the slim volume accepted by a publisher and a reasonable sum of money offered for it was not only an achievement, but also a terrific thrill. At least now he could claim to be a published writer.

He and Clive danced around the sitting room together. They had been happy to get this house in such a quiet spot but near enough to the Art Galleries with its wonderful paintings and book shop and restaurant.

Unfortunately, their happiness about the house was being spoiled by the attitude of some of the neighbours. So far, the Pakistanis hadn't bothered them. Nor had the Kellys at number one, or the McIvors at number two. They weren't sure about Mrs Gardner at number six. Somehow they didn't trust her, were almost afraid of her. The snobby woman with the double-barrelled name at number five was obviously offensive. But the neighbour at number seven had been trying to make their lives miserable. A minister of religion of all people, the Reverend Denby, had been not only nasty but abusive. According to him, they were an abomination in the sight of God, and a dirty one at that. There had been a lump of shit through their letter box and they were sure that the reverend gentleman was responsible. Only the other day, as they were returning from work, he had been in his garden and had called over to them, 'Dirty poofs!'

A minister, of all people! It was truly terrible. They'd attended church where they'd lived before. They just sat quietly in a back pew but people smiled at them in passing, and the minister there, the Reverend MacAndrews, was always very kind and welcoming. But this minister was anything but welcoming. It made them sad.

They had always tried to be good-living Christians. They recited their prayers down on their knees beside their bed every night.

Our Father, which art in heaven,
Hallowed be thy name.
Thy Kingdom come. Thy will be done
On earth as it is in heaven.
Give us this day our daily bread
Forgive us our trespasses as we forgive those who
    trespass against us.
Lead us not into temptation
But deliver us from evil.
For this is the power and the glory
For ever and ever, for Jesus' sake.
Amen

It was the 'Forgive us our trespasses as we forgive those who trespass against us' that they found most difficult. Forgiving people like the snobby woman was bad enough, but a minister of religion like the Reverend Denby was very difficult indeed. A real challenge to their Christian beliefs. But as long as they had each other and their deep, enduring love, they would survive.

Their favourite quotation from the Bible was from Corinthians 13, versus 4-8.

Love is patient, love is kind.
Love is not jealous or boastful.
It is not arrogant or rude.
Love does not insist on its own way, it is not irritable or
    resentful.

They did love one another and Paul said to Clive, 'Don't worry. I'll not allow that terrible hypocrite of a minister, or anyone else, to harm you. Depend on me.'

And Clive did.

They often read the verse about love and quietly recited to themselves,

It does not rejoice at wrong,
But rejoices in the right.
Love bears all things,
Believes all things,
Hopes all things,
Endures all things.
Love never ends.

They did not believe in the Old Testament. But the Reverend Denby obviously did. Paul said the Old Testament, for the most part, was just a collection of stories written by men with over-active and over-dramatic imaginations. But he got depressed at how his novels kept being rejected.

Clive had always tried to encourage Paul's belief in himself and his creative talent, especially when his novels were rejected.

'Every writer, and every painter too, has to suffer lots of rejections. Poor old Van Gogh never sold one painting while he was alive – and as far as writers are concerned . . .

He reeled off all the rejections that now famous novelists had suffered and how they had gone on, despite them, to succeed.

Together, they would succeed. One day they would become famous. They always managed to convince each other of this. A million times, they thanked God for each other, and for the deep love that sustained them and which, like their love for God, would never end.

After they had moved into number four Waterside Way, something occurred to Clive.

'Paul, why don't you make your next novel about the prejudices and discrimination gay men have to suffer.'

'What? It would never be allowed to see the light of day. The chances are that publishers are as prejudiced as most other people, or even worse. They would discriminate by tossing the manuscript straight back at me.'

'Now, you don't know that, Paul. We don't really know anything at all about publishers. They might welcome a book on such a subject.'

'We didn't know what we were about to suffer here, Clive. Before we came here, we thought it was worth a try. A lovely quiet, almost secret kind of place. What could possibly go wrong here? But here we are again, suffering the usual . . .' He shook his head. 'I can never understand, can you? I mean, we've never done anyone any harm.'

'I know. All we've ever tried to do was to be nice and friendly to folk.'

'Yes, and trying to keep ourselves to ourselves didn't work either. So to hell with them.'

'Now, now, Paul. Remember – '"Forgive us our trespasses as we forgive those who trespass against us."'

Paul sighed.

'It's awful difficult trying to be a Christian, isn't it?'

'Yes, but at least we're not suffering as much as poor Jesus did.'

'We don't have his courage though.'

'But we have faith in him. He'll be with us always, supporting us and protecting us from all evil.'

'I don't know about that, Clive. I mean, that snobby woman surely can't be a Christian and that horrible man can't be a true believer in Jesus and his teachings. Love thy neighbour, and all that. We're their neighbours.'

'You're forgetting something, Paul. Forgetting a lot of things. We have so much more in our lives, so much to be thankful for. There's our interesting jobs and at least a few nice colleagues at work. And think of all the students you have helped, who are grateful to you. We don't need to worry about this wee row of houses.'

'Now, you know fine, Clive, it's not just here in this row of houses that we've suffered.'

'All I'm saying is that we have to look at the broader picture and thank God that everyone isn't the same. We're lucky really.'

'Lucky?'

'Of course we are. What about our creative talent.'

'Well at least you're right about that. I can hardly wait to visit the National Gallery and admire your painting there, Clive. I'm more excited about going through to Edinburgh to visit the National Gallery and admire your painting than I am about getting my poetry published.'

'And I'm more excited about you getting your poems accepted then I am about seeing my painting in the National Gallery.'

Paul laughed. 'You liar, you!'

'No, honestly, Paul. I'm really happy for you. But I know that it's a novel you really want to get published and you will be a successful novelist one day. I just know it. You are so talented. I'm proud of you. And I'll love you to the end of time.'

Paul laughed as they embraced.

'Sounds as if I could get a poem out of that. I'll love you to the end of time.'

'Don't mock me, Paul. I mean it.'

'Sorry. How about us taking a walk up to the Galleries, having a meal there and then a walk around? That's one thing

I do like about here. It's such a quiet place. I don't think for a minute that people milling about at the back entrance to the Galleries will even know that the houses are here. Looking down from the Galleries you can't see them for the trees on that side of the river.'

'I know. I don't regret coming here. Do you?'

'No, and despite our awful neighbours!'

'They might not all be awful. Jack Kelly, the police officer in number one, seems a decent sort and the McIvors in number two. And I bet our next door neighbours, the Pakistanis, will be fine. They've probably suffered plenty of prejudice and discrimination themselves and so they'll be able to understand and sympathise.'

'You're right. I'm looking forward to meeting them. Come on, we might as well enjoy the rest of the evening at the Art Galleries.'

Then they happily set off.

10

Clive and Paul walked hastily through the park area on the left and made their way towards the front of the Art Galleries. There were two or three groups of rowdy teenagers wearing wide flared trousers and Rod Stewart's 'Maggie May' was blaring out from a wireless. The youths could be looking for trouble. Usually, they fought among themselves, jeering and shouting at one another, but Clive and Paul were always nervous in case they'd turn on them. They had been feeling uneasy about another couple of men hanging about near Waterside Way – dawdling behind the trees. As soon as the men saw Clive and Paul, they hurried away.

'Who on earth are they, I wonder?' Clive said. 'A right tough-looking pair. Did you see the tattoos one of them had? The other one's bomber jacket looked very worse for wear.'

'Well, at least they're not interested in us, thank goodness. I don't like the look of them though. Shifty kind of characters. They're up to no good, I bet.'

'Well, if they're burglars looking for a house to burgle, they're in for a shock with a police officer living in one of them.'

Paul laughed.

'I hope they do pick his house. Serve them right!'

While walking around the Galleries admiring all the paintings, they came across one of a woman with a cape of long, reddish blonde hair.

'Look,' Clive pointed out. 'Who does that remind you of?'

'Sandra Arlington-Jones, of course. Both Sandra and that Pakistani boy, Mirza Shafaatulla, had better be careful. Mirza and Sandra are both in one of my classes. Mirza's a really clever lad but he obviously dotes on Sandra. Her mother will have a fit if she finds out – a right snobby bitch.'

'I know. She didn't manage to get us chucked out of our house though.'

'What do you think of her neighbour, Mrs Jean Gardner?'

'I wouldn't trust her as far as I could throw her.'

After their walk around the Galleries, they decided to go into town for a visit to the Stirling's Library. They loved to wander around the city centre, admiring Glasgow's wonderful architecture. They especially admired the architecture of the Stirling's Library which had originally been built as a house for one of the wealthy Glasgow Tobacco Lords. Both being artistic, they could admire the Corinthian pillars on the facade and the cupola above.

It was with reluctance that they made their way back home. Not because they didn't like where they lived, not even because of the trouble-making Mrs Arlington-Jones or the smarmy Mrs Jean Gardner. The Reverend Denby was the one they feared and who spoiled the love they had of their nicely situated home and little garden, with a small patch of grass and borders of flowering impatience, french marigolds, primulas and hydrangeas.

'A minister of religion was the last person in the world I thought would be such a danger to us,' Clive said. 'I'm frightened of him.'

'I don't blame you. I've a gut feeling he's going to succeed in doing us real harm if we're not careful.'

'How much more careful can we be? I wonder if we should talk to Jack Kelly. After all, he's been threatening violence against us.'

'He hasn't actually done anything to us though. I mean, he hasn't put a hand on us. It could be said he's just a mad old man and we should simply ignore him.'

'It is frightening though. He's evil. Especially last night, the way he shouted, "Die, die, die" at us. He wants to . . . not just put a hand on us, but kill us.'

'Or have somebody else kill us.'

Clive shuddered. 'For pity's sake, Paul, you and your imagination. Don't make me feel worse.'

Paul put an arm around Clive's shoulders. 'Sorry, but nobody will hurt you if I'm around. I'd die protecting you.'

Tears well up in Clive's eyes. 'I know,' he said, 'I know.'

II

'He's got the true spirit of Scotland, Pop,' Bashir said.

'Who?' Mahmood asked.

'Jimmy Reid.'

'And who is this Jimmy Reid?'

'He's a Clydesider, a ship builder and a union man, a leader and a self-taught intellectual.'

'He is the true spirit of Scotland because he is self-taught? Ah, like me?'

Bashir laughed. 'Yes, OK, Pop. But in a bigger way. I mean, he's taking on Heath's government. Heath wants to close all the shipyards and that would make at least six thousand workers lose their jobs.'

'What can this Jimmy Reid do?'

'It's in all the papers. Instead of going on strike, he's told everyone they're going to have a "work-in". They would fill every order on their books. Look, there it is in the paper.' Bashir read out, '"We are not going to strike. We are not even having a sit-in strike. . . . And there will be no hooliganism, there will be no vandalism, there will be no bevvying, because the world is watching us."'

'No bevvying. That means drinking alcohol, doesn't it?'

'Yes.'

46

'He does sound like a good man,' Mahmood admitted. 'Like a good Muslim. Not like you, Bashir. You drink.'

'Och, just the odd pint, Pop. Anyway, lots of us are getting together to help them. We're trying to gather money, anything we can get,' Bashir said. 'I've put a collection box in the shop. It's to help keep them supplied with food. They're going to be shut in there, working hard, probably for months.'

Mahmood sighed. 'You are a kind man, Bashir. Not a good Muslim, but a kind man. I cannot deny that.'

'Right, I'll speak to the neighbours first.'

Jack Kelly welcomed him into house number one and his wife Mae immediately put the kettle on. Bashir explained his mission.

'Well, the man's got courage, right enough,' Jack agreed. 'And principles. It's a welcome change to read about somebody bringing everyone together in a good cause. I thought after the Ibrox disaster everyone had come together. Rangers and Celtic, Orangemen and Catholics, but the game was hardly over when all the old prejudices and hatred flared up again.'

'All the workers will stick together to the end with a leader like Jimmy Reid.'

'Yes,' Jack said. 'I believe you're right, Bashir. I'll help in any way I can.'

Next Bashir called on the McIvors at number two. Mae Kelly came with him so that she could make sure Doris understood what Bashir had come about.

'She's getting a bit distracted with all the worry and stress of looking after her mother,' Mae explained.

'Och well, maybe I'd better not bother her.'

'No, no, I'm sure she'll be pleased to see you.'

And indeed Doris seemed delighted to welcome them both in.

'I thought it was Mrs Gardner but it's really great to see any of my neighbours. Everyone is so kind.'

'Who's that black man?' old Mrs McIvor called out, much to her daughter's embarrassment.

'Oh, I'm so sorry, Bashir. So very sorry.'

Bashir laughed. 'Don't worry.' Then to Mrs McIvor, 'It's brown, Ma. I've got a brown face.'

The visit to Clive and Paul went very well but Mrs Arlington-Jones and Mrs Gardner were horrified at the mere mention of Jimmy Reid's name. The Reverend Denby was surprisingly welcoming.

'Reid is at least trying,' he agreed. 'No hooliganism, no vandalism and no drinking. I did my best to preach these things over the pulpit but God alone knows how many of my congregation followed my commands.'

Bashir wasn't sure if it was a good thing to have the Reverend Denby on his side. He'd seen the way he treated Clive and Paul. He made for the Art Galleries next with a collection box. On the way, he saw Mirza and Sandra, arms around each other and gazing adoringly at one another.

Oh dear, oh dear, he thought. There's serious trouble brewing there.

12

Bashir was fond of his father-in-law, Mahmood, but he was fond of Mirza too and suffered constantly with a division of loyalties. It would have been so much better and more appropriate if Mirza had fallen in love with a Muslim girl. He was actually too young to be falling in love with anyone. He was just a schoolboy, for goodness sake. There was a Pakistani Muslim girl in his class. Bashir had seen her. A pretty little girl, she was. Why couldn't Mirza have fallen for her? But of course, he knew perfectly well that falling in love wasn't a cold-blooded thing that you planned. 'That's for the best,' you tell yourself. 'I'll have her.' But no, it seldom worked that way.

British people were horrified at the mere idea of Muslim arranged marriages. They thought that they were forced marriages. This was not so. When he'd had a bride chosen for him, for instance, he could have said no.

But he didn't because, for one thing, he trusted his parents to make a good, suitable and happy choice for him, and they did. He had been broken-hearted when the dreadful gas explosion had killed his dear wife, and his loving parents. Naturally, Mahmood had been broken-hearted too. He had lost a much-loved daughter. He would never forget, and he would be eternally grateful to Mahmood for welcoming him into the bosom of his family. He and his wife Rasheeda had treated him like a son. Mirza was like a brother to him. Mirza was only a schoolboy but was a tall, handsome young man, broad-shouldered and muscular, as a result no doubt of the time he spent in the school gym.

Yes, he wished Mirza had made Mahmood happy by bringing the little Pakistani girl home to be introduced to him. At the same time, he couldn't help understanding and sympathising with Mirza when he saw Sandra, the girl Mirza said he loved and wanted to marry.

He truthfully had never seen such a gorgeous girl in his life. She had a smooth creamy skin and a pretty pink rosebud mouth. But it was her hair – my God, talk about a crowning glory! It was long, reaching below her waist, and such a shining red-gold colour, it was startlingly beautiful.

Couldn't Mahmood see and understand how and why Mirza loved such a girl? Sadly, he couldn't and it left Bashir with a worrying dilemma. He wanted to be loyal to Mahmood – one hundred per cent loyal – but try as he might, he couldn't help understanding and sympathising with Mirza.

He tried to talk to Mahmood.

'Pop, look at the girl. Please try to see why Mirza has fallen in love with her. Have you ever seen such a beautiful creature in your life?'

'I'm constantly surprised and disappointed in you, Bashir,' Mahmood said. 'You have developed so many Western ways and even talk like a born Glaswegian and I can understand that in a way, with you working in our Gorbals shop all the time.'

'But, Pop, poor Mirza. I love him like a brother and can't bear to see him so unhappy. Please try to find it in your heart to accept Sandra and Mirza's love for her.'

'No, never, Bashir. And I'm sure that girl's mother will feel the very same as I do. She will not want a mixed marriage for her daughter. They are Christians, Bashir. I have seen her going to church on Sunday mornings with that minister of the Christian religion who lives in the end house.'

Bashir sighed. But he still couldn't help feeling sorry for Mirza. Somehow he had to help him.

13

It was dark.

'Oh God,' Mae groaned. 'Not another power cut.'

That and the strike of the delivery drivers made it impossible to get any bread in the shops. People were forced to walk in the dark to the bake houses, which just worked during the night. They couldn't even use their cars because of the fuel crisis.

'I'll go,' Jack said.

'No, of course you won't – walking all that way with your sore hip. No, I'll go. I'll get Doris to go with me. Her mother gets a strong sleeping tablet at night now, so it's all right to leave her.'

'Are you sure?'

'Yes, of course.'

'All right, but take care.'

She went next door and collected a more than willing Doris who was always glad of any excuse to get out of the house. They ventured arm in arm and treading with great care through the pitch blackness.

Soon they heard footsteps behind them and Mae called out nervously, 'Who's there?'

Then she heard Mirza Shafaatulla's voice. 'It's OK. It's

only me and Sandra. Are you making for the bake house as well?'

'Yes, and I'm just hoping they won't be sold out before we get there. What a carry on, isn't it? Nothing but strikes and cuts nowadays. And I can't understand what this decimal currency is they're talking about next.'

They went on chatting as they slowly walked along.

'Yeah, I know. But not everything is hopeless. That explosion on board Apollo thirteen could have ended in one big disaster.'

'Right enough. We should be thankful for small mercies, as they say.'

The only mercy she'd be thankful for, Mae thought, was getting enough five pound notes together to replace the ones she'd stolen. She could think of nothing else. Now that she was sure she'd seen the robbers, she could imagine how dangerous they could be. A scruffy, tough-looking pair, they were.

What's going to happen? She kept tormenting herself with the same question over and over again. What's going to happen? What am I going to do?

'Oops!' She stumbled and nearly brought Doris down with her. It was only Mirza and Sandra's catching them from behind that saved her.

Everything was so pitch black. Street lamps, house windows – not the slightest glimmer of light anyway; not a chink.

They all linked arms. Sandra said, 'My mother thinks I'm just with you, Mae. You being a police officer's wife means you must be respectable.'

'Oh yes?' Mae laughed but of course she was only too aware of how far from respectability she was. If Mrs Arlington-Jones only knew, how horrified she would be. Anyone would be horrified. I could be arrested, put in jail for what I've done, Mae thought. The robbers obviously took advantage of the then-vacant house to break in easily and stash the money. Imagine their surprise upon returning to find that it was now occupied – and by a police officer! But now Mae was just as guilty. She should have reported the discovery straight away. To take such a large sum of money without questioning its origin was no trivial matter.

The worst thing was the shame it would bring on Jack. Jack Kelly had always been so straight and honest. No police officer had been more admired. In fact, he deserved a medal for what he'd done during the Ibrox disaster alone.

Oh Jack, I'm sorry, Mae kept thinking. I'm so sorry.

14

The thought of her husband Jack's fury if he ever found out made Mae Kelly's heart beat through her body at such an uneven rate that she thought she was going to have a heart attack. Over and over again, all sorts of scenarios formed in her mind. What if the robbers came to the house – despite having seen Jack in his police uniform? They could find out he was on day shift and come during his working hours. What then?

If they found out that most of the money had gone, they would think Jack was helping himself. They'd come to that conclusion, knowing that it had not been reported to the police station. Then what? Would the robbers phone or write anonymously to the police station accusing Jack? She had been saving as much as she could and replacing as many of the notes as she could but she hadn't managed to replace nearly enough of it yet.

It was impossible to sleep and she lay watching the darkness as it filtered into cold grey gauze. The furniture of the bedroom appeared like menacing ghosts – the tall wardrobe, the squat dressing table, the basket chair – glistening faintly. The luminous alarm clock beat an endless tattoo in her head. She thought if she didn't sleep, she'd go mad and when morning came, her nerves were stretched to breaking point.

When Jack asked for an extra egg with his breakfast, she snapped at him, 'That's all you ever think about – food. It's all you care about. That and your stupid car.'

Jack's jaw muscles tightened.

'What's up with your face this morning. You're glad enough of the Mini when it takes you to the seaside or collects you and brings you home from visits to your friends.'

She felt so distracted with worry, she just wanted him to get out of her sight and leave. He stormed away without kissing her. She longed to run after him, apologise and plead with him to come back. Instead she wandered about the quiet house, making herself another cup of tea and trying to work out what she could do. It was then she suddenly thought of a moneylender. She remembered seeing a moneylender's office near where they used to live.

Her heart leapt with apprehension at the mere idea but she had to do something, and quickly. She flung on her coat, grabbed her handbag and hurried from the house. It was a bright, sunny morning and buildings were silhouetted, coffee-coloured, against the glassy blue sky. She ran for a bus and once at her destination, she crossed the road and hurried towards the moneylender's office, believing that she really had gone mad. What was the procedure in such a place? Did they ask her for references? Or some sort of security? She had no idea. Then suddenly she was startled by a familiar voice.

'Hello there! Searching the shops for an expensive new outfit, are you, while your poor old man's working his butt off in the station?'

It was one of Jack's police pals that he entertained to dinner every Sunday.

She couldn't bring herself to fake a laugh. But she managed to say, 'Caught in the act. A lovely morning, isn't it?' Then she gave him a wave as she hastened away. Further down the street, she surreptitiously looked back. Now there were two police officers strolling along together, obviously on duty. No way could she risk returning to the money-lender's office.

Eventually, home again, she shut the door and leaned her head and back against it. Such anguish of mind couldn't continue. She knew that. She would simply have to tell Jack. There was nothing else she could do. He arrived home and he was barely inside the door when she burst into tears.

'Mae!' He gathered her into his arms and smoothed a straggle of hair away from her wet face. 'What on earth's wrong with you these days? You're not yourself at all.'

'Oh Jack,' she sobbed. 'I'm in an awful mess. Darling, I'm sorry. I didn't mean it but the cost of living's so terrible and money disappears so quickly and sometimes I just don't know what to do.'

'All right, all right. There's no need to get into such a state.'

'But Jack . . .'

He pressed a finger to her mouth, silencing her. 'Just keep quiet for a minute and let me think. Well, it won't be easy, but yes, I think I could stretch to another couple of pounds a week on your housekeeping money.'

'But Jack . . .'

'No more buts, and no more tragic faces. I mean it. Now, just be quiet. I'll manage it somehow. But for God's sake, Mae, try and be a bit more careful. I'm not made of money. Now, come on. Get a grip of yourself and stop this nonsense. It was bad enough this morning when you were really nasty to me.'

She mopped her face, avoiding his eyes.

'I'm sorry.'

It was no use.

'Come on then, what's for dinner. I'm starving,' Jack said.

She tried to tell herself that Jack meant well. Often he'd said, 'You're a great wee manager.' He really believed he was being generous giving her a paltry raise in her housekeeping money.

She wanted to tell him, 'Those extra pounds won't even pay for your next steak dinner. I don't know what to do. For God's sake, help me.'

But she didn't. He was as straight as a die and such a hard, conscientious worker and so positive and cheerful, despite the agony he obviously suffered with his injured hip.

She loved him and nothing had ever spoiled their happiness before. Many a happy time they'd had together. Especially during the summer in Jack's pride and joy of a car with its fancy rims and hub caps and jazzy seat covers. When Jack was off duty, she often helped him to polish the car.

'Right,' Jack repeated. 'Where's my dinner then?'

He kissed her and she clung round his neck, not wanting to let him go.

Laughing, he disentangled himself from her arms.

'Later. First things first and that means a nice big juicy steak.'

15

As Paul said – to be a writer, especially a novelist, you had to be interested in people and what made them tick. You had to get around and observe people. Clive said it was much the same in art, at least the observing bit. And so, as much as they could, they went around observing and discussing what they'd seen and heard.

The West End was always fascinating, with Byres Road and the lanes, including Ashton Lane, leading off it. The people going about in that area were mostly young university students.

Just up from Byres Road were the Botanic Gardens and Clive and Paul enjoyed a walk around, then stretched out on the grass for a while before enjoying a visit to the big glass Kibble Palace. It was lovely that it was now the school summer holiday time and so they were in no rush. They took a bus into the centre of town and then walked down Buchanan Street.

Clive said, 'I always tell people who come to visit Glasgow to keep looking up. That way they don't miss the beautiful architecture of the buildings.'

'Yes, and I doubt if there's anywhere else that has so much, if any, of that warm red sandstone.'

There were the steps leading up to the Concert Hall at the

top of Buchanan Street, all shaped in a half circle and covered by a rainbow of young people sitting laughing and chatting together. Further down, there were fashionable shops to visit but Clive and Paul preferred a leisurely stroll down the street, watching and listening to all the buskers.

There were two young men in kilts, one playing the bagpipes, the other rattling on the drums. Several men from Peru in huge feathered headdresses and loose leather coats were playing pan pipes and drums.

Then there was the St Petersburg brass band. Further down again, several Scotsmen in what seemed to be ancient tartan cloaks wound around their bodies and under their legs pranced about. The street led right down to the busy Argyle Street, but first Clive and Paul wandered round George Square.

Clive and Paul got the bus back up Sauchiehall Street and walked through the park, before returning to Waterside Way.

They were shocked and saddened at the situation developing in the park. Youths were lolling about drinking from bottles of wine and Buckfast – or Buckie as they called it. Many of the drinkers looked under-age. Fights sometimes broke out between gangs. Clive and Paul had also heard that drugs had been found on many of the youths. Before now, they had even seen youths urinating in the park.

'It used to be such a beautiful, respectable place,' Clive said. 'If it gets any worse, we won't be able to walk through it. It won't be safe enough. Especially for the likes of us.'

'I saw in the paper yesterday that there's been a man convicted of harassing a poor guy and shouting, "Homosexuality is a sin against Jesus."'

'Sounds like the Reverend Denby.'

'Yeah. There's still too many of his kind around. I wish they would do something to make the park a safer place. There's so many angry youths, just looking for a meeting place to drink and start trouble.'

'I often wonder what their parents are thinking of. Don't they know what their children are up to?'

'Probably they don't care. The chances are they're out drinking or getting stupid on drugs themselves.'

'I've said it before and I'll say it again. We've been lucky, Paul. Remember our mothers and fathers. Well, not so much our fathers, but our mothers were always loving and loyal.'

'Yeah. One of my earliest memories is of a neighbour coming to my mother – I couldn't have been more than six. Anyway, I remember this neighbour saying to my mother, "Do you know your boy's a poof?" And my mother said, "My boy's a good wee boy and I love him and I always will."'

'That was the same kind of woman my mother was – bless her. And it was her – like your mother – who taught me to be a good Christian. My mother used to go down on her knees with me beside my bed and recite the Lord's Prayer with me.'

'Yeah. Brave women too, weren't they?'

'Yes, they were. We must always try to have as much courage as them, Paul.'

And they continued their walk through the park, ignoring the violence around them.

16

Mae didn't know what good it would do but she felt an urgency to go to the Art Galleries. She might find out something. At the back of her mind, of course, was the thought that while she was out of the house and Jack was at work, the robbers would come, break into the house and find the money gone. But what good would that do? She didn't know but she was even more fearful of the robbers arriving when she was in the house. She had to get away and decided to ask Doris if she'd like to accompany her for a walk and a visit to the Art Galleries.

Doris thought it was a great idea. So without wasting a minute, they set off, with Doris holding on to one side of old Mrs McIvor and Mae holding on to her other arm.

'I just thought,' Mae explained to Doris, 'that it would do both of you good to get out for a wee turn and some fresh air. Then after we've walked round to the Art Galleries, we can have a cup of tea in the café. It would be good for you and interesting if we could walk round and see some of the exhibits but maybe your mother wouldn't have enough energy for that.'

'What?' Doris rolled her eyes. 'She's got more energy than both of us put together. It's only her mind that's gone, poor thing.'

There was no problem walking round to the Art Galleries. Indeed, the old woman, to all appearances, seemed to enjoy the experience and gazed happily around at the trees in the park and up at the beautiful architecture of the building.

Mae didn't like the look of some of the youths hanging about in the park, however, and it was then that she remembered Jack saying something about the police trying to crack down on the under-age drinking and drug abuse in the parks. She told Doris about what she'd learned as they strolled away.

'Gosh,' Doris said. 'It's obviously fascinating being married to a police officer. You hear everything that's going on.' Her eyes twinkled mischievously. 'And particularly fascinating when he's such a handsome police officer.'

Mae managed a laugh. 'Yes, I can't deny he's a handsome police officer. I'm very lucky.'

Although she felt anything but lucky at that moment. Reaching the Art Galleries, she said, 'Do you want a cup of tea now or a look around the gift shop first?'

'Let's look at the gift shop. We've plenty of time for the tea. It's ages since Mother and I have been in the gift shop. It's a bit much for me to manage her outside on my own.'

'Well, I can have a walk round to the Art Galleries with you any day. Your mother seems to be enjoying it as well. So it'll do us all good.'

'Wonderful!'

In the gift shop, Mae looked over at the pay counter and wondered where the robbers had got the money. The robbery couldn't have happened during the day. There had been no reports in the newspapers of an armed hold-up and Jack would have mentioned it if there had been anything dramatic like that. So it must have been under cover of darkness and probably from a safe somewhere nearby. Or under the counter? She sidled round to one side in an effort to look behind it but wasn't successful. The place was busy and there were several assistants crushed together, serving a queue of customers.

Doris, still clinging on to her mother, was happily admiring all sorts of articles on display. Suddenly, Mae felt guilty and hurried over to take Mrs McIvor's other arm.

Doris said, 'This is great. Even Mother is interested and enjoying looking at all the lovely gifts. She's never been so quiet and well-behaved for ages.'

'It's the colours and sparkle of everything. There are so many gorgeous things. Copies of paintings, and exhibits, and look at that jewelry.'

Doris said, 'It's so wonderful to have Mother quiet like this. I confess I often feel like murdering her when she keeps repeating things over and over again at me. It drives me absolutely frantic at times.'

'It's understandable, Doris. But it shows you that you need to get out and about more.'

'I do too,' Mae thought. She was afraid to be in the house, that was her problem. What would the robbers do if they found the money had gone? She was going to save up as hard as she could and as fast as she could, to replace all the five pound notes.

But that had not happened yet and so she believed she had good reason to be afraid. Very afraid indeed.

17

'It did your mother and you so much good to get out and have a bit of fresh air and exercise,' Mae told Doris later that week. 'So let's do it again another day. We can take an arm each and have a walk around the park, then go to the Art Galleries as we did before. You must get bored stuck in the house so much.'

'Gosh, I do. That would be wonderful, Mae.'

'Well, come on. No time like the present.'

So after Doris had smoothed her mother's glossy white hair with a brush and secured it with a couple of kirby grips, they set off.

Mae was afraid to be in the house by herself in case the robbers broke in. At the same time, she was glad to be able to help Doris and her mother.

Once more, Doris and Mae were pleased and relieved at how well-behaved the old woman was during their walk. Mrs McIvor gazed at everything with obvious interest and pleasure. There were no violent struggles.

Doris said, 'Poor old thing. She must get bored as well.'

'Would you look at that.' Mae indicated a crowd of youngsters hunkered down and passing a bottle of wine from one mouth to another. 'They can't even have reached their teens.'

'Surely their mothers don't know what they're up to.'

'Jack says most of the mothers are either alkies or drug addicts.'

'Alkies?'

'Alcoholics.'

Doris sighed. 'My mother was always so good to me. She just lived for me and Alec, when we needed her. That's why I try to be as good to her now that she needs me.'

'You keep saying that, Doris, but you're going to ruin your health and be of no use to your mother or to anyone soon. You wrote to him again, didn't you? A pleading letter?'

'Yes.'

'Well, once your brother arrives, he'll see for himself what's needed. He'll get your mother into a good nursing home. She won't be bored there, Doris. She'll be happy and well-cared for, as I've already told you several times.'

'You're right, Mae. My health's cracking up with the strain of never being able to relax and even get a decent sleep at night. Goodness, look over there.'

Several youths had begun to fight and Mae saw the flash of razors.

'Let's get out of here. And as quick as we can.'

They hurried away in the direction of the Art Galleries. Once they had safely arrived there, Doris said, 'I remember that park being so peaceful and respectable. What a difference now.'

'Jack says it's going to be sorted out soon. He says a clear message is going to be sent to gang members or anybody misbehaving in Kelvingrove Park – we'll come after you.'

'Well, I hope they do. One thing's for sure, Mae. You're never likely to be bored, married to a police officer. And he's so handsome too. I've never seen such a handsome man.'

'So you keep telling me.'

'Oh dear, am I getting as bad as my mother and repeating myself all the time? I'm sorry, Mae.'

'It's all right. I was just joking.'

She was wondering what else Jack would tell her about the men who'd robbed the Art Galleries.

18

They were waiting for him at the beginning of Waterside Way, blocking his path to the house. They were a group of white youths in expensive school uniforms. They were the sons of wealthy businessmen – owners of supermarkets and whole-sale warehouses, company directors, doctors, professionals and consultants. Mirza was returning from school with Zaida, Sandra, Maq and Ali. He'd invited his pals Maq and Ali home for a meal.

'Get lost,' one of the youths said to the girls and to Maq and Ali. 'It's him we want,' indicating Mirza.

'You get lost,' Mirza said, 'you bunch of pathetic cowards. I'll take on every one of you in a fair one-to-one fight.'

Sandra said, 'What's the big idea? What do you expect to gain by picking on Mirza?'

'We're here to warn this fuckin' bastard to keep clear of a white girl like you.'

Sandra's voice loudened indignantly. 'I choose to be with whoever I like. And I choose to be with Mirza. You can all beat it and mind your own business.'

Zaida said, 'Sandra, you just go home. I'll stay with Mirza. Maq and Ali, you go and wait at our house.'

'No way,' Maq and Ali said. 'We're staying with you and

Mirza.' And then to the tight mob barring their way, 'You're a bunch of cowards, the lot of you. You haven't the nerve to have a one-to-one fight with Mirza. He'd flatten any of you.'

'What's going on here?' a voice called out behind the youths. They turned and saw two policemen coming towards Waterside Way. Mirza recognised them as friends of Jack Kelly at house number one.

Sandra called back, 'They're stopping us getting into Waterside Way and our houses. They don't belong here.'

One of the youths said, 'We were just having a laugh.'

'Well,' one of the policemen told him, 'away and have a laugh somewhere else. You're blocking the way.'

'Sure, no problem.'

They all began to swagger off but one of them called back to Mirza, 'See you again soon.'

Once in Waterside Way, Maq said to Mirza, 'Maybe you should cool it and not be seen so much with Sandra. They're obviously determined to get you if you carry on like this – always being with her.'

'Whose side are you on?' Mirza protested indignantly.

'Yours, of course. But I don't want you beaten and kicked to a pulp and maybe even killed by a mob like that. We can't always be here to help you and a couple of policemen aren't likely to turn up again either.'

Sandra said, 'Jack Kelly's a policeman. We could at least tell him or his wife, Mae. They know about Mirza and me and they're all right about us. They could at least keep an eye on things, warn them off or something. I don't know, but at least we could ask for their advice. They know for a start that we can't make an official report to the police station. My mother would find out about Mirza and me and then all hell would be let loose.'

'And my father!' Mirza said. 'It's bloody damnable, isn't it?'

'How about Bashir?' Zaida asked.

'I know he would help but what can he do? That crowd are liable to turn up anywhere and any time, determined to get me. Bashir, or anyone else, can't know where and when their next stupid attack is going to be.'

Maq suddenly brightened. 'We could get a gang together.'

'Start a race war, you mean?'

'No, I didn't mean anything racial.'

'That's how it would look. White guys from a posh private school, sons of wealthy and influential parents, and coloured guys like us. We'd get all the blame and I can just see the newspaper headlines – "They're not wanted in Britain. Send them back home to their own country." etc, etc.'

'Och, you don't know that. We could just meet their mob and batter the living daylights out of them. The chances are that would finish them for good. They would never try anything again. End of story.'

Mirza sighed.

'I don't think so, Maq, but I appreciate how you're trying to help. You're a real pal. But I think, first of all, we'd be better to try the talking bit. Talk to the Kellys and to Bashir and see what they say. OK?'

Maq shrugged.

'OK. It's worth a try, I suppose. But if they don't come up with a better idea, I can still get a gang together and we could try that.'

Ali spoke then. 'I'll go along with whatever's decided on to help you, Mirza. You know that.'

'Yes. The pair of you have always been my best friends and I'm really grateful to you both.'

They all began walking along Waterside Way. Maq, Ali and Zaida turned into number three. Mirza waited with Sandra.

'In you go,' he told the others. 'I won't be a minute.'

'For God's sake.' Sandra became agitated. 'Go in with them.

70

Your father will see us. Or my mother might come out at any moment.'

'I'm getting sick of all this. I'm not a coward. I can face my father and your mother.'

'No, no,' Sandra cried out. 'That would be the end of us. They'd make sure of it. I couldn't bear it.'

Suddenly Mirza caught her in his arms and kissed her passionately. She struggled, broke away from him with a moan and raced along the Way to house number five.

It was fortunate, as she told Mirza at school next day, that her mother had been in the kitchen and had not seen them.

'But after this, I'm not going to walk home with you from school. I can't bear the suspense of either my mother or her friend next door or that awful Reverend Denby seeing us. At least we can see each other at school.'

'We're doing this extra study course just now but what about the rest of the school holidays?' Mirza asked. 'Do we not see each other at all then?'

'We'll find somewhere safe to meet. There must be somewhere safe.'

'Oh Sandra, I need you.'

'And I need you. But we'll have to be patient for a bit longer. Once we get to university, it should be easier. Nothing must happen to spoil your career chances, Mirza. Remember the teacher said you had a brilliant career in front of you, if you got to university and worked hard for your degree.

Mirza sighed. 'You need your degree too.'

'Yes, and I'm going to work hard to get it. And what'll help to keep me going is knowing that at the end of it, we'll be able to get married. We'll just have to be patient.'

'I don't know if I can be patient for much longer, Sandra. I'm beginning to feel like an unexploded bomb.'

71

19

It seemed incredible to Mae that Jack was able to chat away to her as if nothing had happened, as if her distress had simply melted away after he'd given her the couple of pounds raise in her housekeeping money.

Now he was telling her about the plan for the opening of a pedestrian area in Buchanan Street. 'Everybody will be able to walk around freely without the noise and danger of traffic,' he explained enthusiastically. 'I've read all about it. They're going to replace the parking meters with plants and shrubs in what is now one of Glasgow's main traffic arteries.'

'Really?' She struggled to put interest into her tone of voice.

'Yes. At first it will only be enforced from eleven in the morning to four in the afternoon, but if it proves popular traffic could be banished from the entire street!'

'Goodness.'

'I thought you'd be more excited – you can do all your shopping with no distraction and in a much calmer environment.'

'Well that's nice.'

Nothing on earth was further from her thoughts. All their wonderful plans could sink to the bottom of the river, for all she cared. She felt as if she was sinking herself – alone and drowning. What was she going to do? How could she go on like this?

She only forgot at night when she was gripped in Jack's strong arms and his lips and hands were caressing every part of her body. Her heart raced then but with pleasurable excitement, not terror. Her body pulsated with the thrill of him entering her. She wanted the forgetfulness, the pleasurable excitement, to last forever. But with the light of morning, and especially after Jack had left for work and she was alone, the terror returned.

She didn't know what to do. More and more, she depended on Doris for company. Doris was more than happy to have her visit or to accompany her and her mother on some outing. Doris was fascinated when she recounted all that Jack had told her about the future plans for Glasgow.

'Gosh, Mae, I can hardly wait until all that happens. We could go shopping together, couldn't we?'

'Of course, if you wanted to.'

'That would be wonderful, Mae. It'll give me something else to look forward to. And if Mother lives long enough to see it, she would be fascinated too. The only time she's quiet and well-behaved is when she's out somewhere with you. Otherwise – well, you know yourself what she's like in the house.'

Indeed Mae did, and she often thought that she'd go stark raving mad if she had to put up with the old woman's stupid repetitive talk and awful behaviour. All right, the poor soul was ill with dementia but it was terribly hard for Doris. Her mother was always running away from the house day and night and Doris had to chase after her and haul her back from nearly falling in the river or disappearing elsewhere. Doris seldom got a night's sleep. The old woman didn't seem to need a whole night's sleep and as often as not, despite her sleeping tablet, she was up in the middle of the night and away outside, wearing only her nightie.

'I always worry that, apart from anything else,' Doris said, 'she'll get her death of cold. But not her. It's me that gets the cold.'

Mae worried about Doris. She had grown painfully thin and gaunt and her grey-streaked hair stuck up like a wild neglected brush.

'You need to look after yourself more, Doris.'

'How can I?' Doris looked as if she was about to break into wild sobbing and Mae realised it was a stupid thing to say. How could poor Doris ever be able to look after herself?

'I'm sure your brother will soon come over and help you in every way he can. Now that you've written to him again.'

Nevertheless, in comparison with Doris, she was lucky. She tried to keep telling herself that. But it didn't work.

20

Another day, Mae Kelly was hurrying back from doing some urgent shopping when she saw old Mrs McIvor pulling and tugging at the handle of number one. She began to run towards the house. Obviously Mrs McIvor had got out of her own house and was too confused to get back in to the right one again.

'Mrs McIvor, it's Mae,' she cried out as soon as she reached the house. 'Mae Kelly. Come on, I'll take you into your own place.'

But Mrs McIvor pushed her away. 'She's locked me out.'

'No dear, she hasn't.'

'Who are you? What do you know?'

'I'm Mae Kelly. Your next door neighbour. You've met me before. Remember?'

'No, I don't. I don't know who you are. She's locked me out.'

Just then, Jack's car arrived.

'Something wrong? Can I help?' He struggled out of the car and limped towards them. He knew about Mrs McIvor. Mae had told him how poor Doris suffered because of the old woman's dementia.

It was then that the door of number two was flung open

and a wild-haired Doris hastened out in great agitation.

'I just went to the bathroom. I must have forgotten to lock the door. Oh, I'm so sorry.'

'Not to worry,' Jack said, linking arms with the old woman. 'Come on, I'll see you safely in to your own home.'

Mrs McIvor said to Doris, 'I got the police to you.'

Mae went into the house with Doris and the old woman. Jack went back to garage his car.

'I won't be long,' Mae called after him.

Inside number two, Doris was trembling and almost in tears.

'Oh Mae, I forgot to lock the door. Do you think I'm going the same way as my mother? Is it genetic, do you think?'

'Of course not. You're under a terrible strain, Doris. I don't know how you manage as well as you do.'

'I'll get the police to you,' Mrs McIvor said.

'Oh God,' Doris groaned, rubbing a hand through her hair and making it even frizzier and messier. 'She's found something else to keep repeating at me.'

'I'll get the police to you.'

'Doris, something will have to be done,' Mae said firmly. 'You definitely can't go on like this. It's enough to drive anyone crazy. Forgive me for saying this, Doris, but even I feel like punching her in the mouth to make her shut up. And I only see her occasionally.'

'She wasn't always like this. She was such a good mother to me and Alec. I must never forget that.'

'But you've got to face it, Doris. She's not that woman any more. It's sad, I know, but for her own good as well as yours, something will have to be done.'

'More and more, I feel like being violent to her myself.' Doris began to moan and weep and Mae put a comforting arm around her. 'I'm so ashamed, Mae, but what can I do?'

'You'll have to do the best thing for your mother and that means getting her into a good nursing home now.'

Mrs McIvor was wandering in and out of the room. 'I'll get the police to you.'

'I suppose you're right. But I've wanted so much to look after her with the patience and love she always gave me. I felt I owed it to her.'

'It's too much for you, Doris. Far too much. You know it is. The very best thing for your mother now is to get her into a good nursing home. You can visit her every day. And she'd be happy there. She'd have company and be well looked after. She'd be much happier, I'm sure. And you'd be happier too.'

'But what'll Alec say?'

'Oh, for pity's sake, Doris. Give me his address. I'll write to him and tell him the desperate urgency of the situation. I'll tell him that if he doesn't respond and do something, I'll get the police – something desperate like that. I'll think of some kind of threat.'

'You've done so much for me already, Mae. Would you really write and tell him the truth about how Mum is?'

'Of course.'

Doris wiped at her eyes. 'All right. I'll wait until he gets your letter.'

'I'll write the letter tonight and post it tomorrow. But Doris, are you sure you'll be all right until you hear from him?'

'I'll get the police to you.'

'Yes, all right, Mum.' Doris spoke to her mother through gritted teeth and made Mae all the more worried about leaving her.

'Are you sure you'll be all right, Doris? Look, I'll wait until you give your mother her medication. Give her an extra dose to make her sleep.'

Doris nodded and went to fetch the necessary tablets. At least her mother dutifully swallowed them over. Mae waited until the old woman was nodding off to sleep and then she helped Doris tuck her safely into bed.

'Thank you so much.' Doris's voice trembled as she saw Mae to the door. Mae gave her an affectionate hug.

'Everything's going to be all right soon. Just cling to that thought.'

Once back in her own house, she wished she had such a thought to cling to. She was sure Doris's life was bound to get better. Her own life was sinking into the abyss of hell.

She was desperately trying to gather five pound notes but was she going to have enough before the robbers broke in?

21

Mahmood had not minded in the slightest when his young son Mirza asked if he could bring Sandra Arlington-Jones in for tea. Indeed, he had been delighted.

'Welcome. Welcome,' he'd told Mirza and then Sandra. His wife Rasheeda had made a nice cup of tea for their young guest and also produced a plate of assorted biscuits. Biscuits were a very popular seller in his grocery shop. Western people liked biscuits and Sandra had been no exception. She had a healthy young person's appetite and enjoyed several.

But then Mahmood had become worried. Mirza had settled himself at Sandra's feet and gazed adoringly up at her.

Eventually Mahmood spoke to Mirza about it.

'Mirza, you must remember that we are Muslims. You can never be anything more than friends to any Christian woman.'

'Father, you are prejudiced and I am not. I'll be more than friends with who I like, whether she's Christian or not. And eventually, when I'm older, if all goes well, I'll marry who I like, whether she's Christian or not.'

Mahmood was horrified. 'No, no, my son. You cannot do that. Your mother and I will choose a wife for you, even if it means we have to go to Pakistan to do so.'

'Father, this is Scotland and I'm nearly seventeen. In Scotland, anyone can get married as young as sixteen. It's the law.'

Mahmood felt a cauldron of emotion begin to boil up inside his small frame. Anger, disappointment, grief. He was completely appalled.

'You can't even think of disobeying your parents and your religion. It is not possible.'

'Anything's possible, Father, and now that you've brought up the subject, I confess – I love Sandra Arlington-Jones and I hope one day to marry her.'

'You're being ridiculous, Mirza. Isn't he being ridiculous, Rasheeda?'

'Yes, of course. You haven't even known her long enough to be friends.'

'I've known her a lot longer than you think. She's lived at number five for years but I knew her before we came to live in Waterside Way. We go to the same school.'

Mahmood said, 'I forbid you to see her again.'

Mirza managed a laugh. 'Father, we're in the same class at school.'

'At school, you will concentrate on your lessons, then you will come straight home alone. Or with your sister, Zaida, only. If you do not do that, your mother will wait at the school gate and then escort you home.'

'For God's sake!' Mirza groaned.

'Do not blaspheme, you wicked boy. If necessary, I will speak to the girl's mother.'

'Oh no, Father. No, please don't do that.'

Mahmood experienced a welcome surge of relief at the sight of Mirza's distress. He had found what was needed to bring Mirza back to his senses.

'Very well. We'll wait and see how you behave, Mirza. If

you obey the wishes of your father, all will be well. If you do not obey . . .' His shoulders raised in a shrug and he spread out his hands.

Mirza now sat tight-lipped, pale-faced and silent.

'So,' Mahmood said firmly, 'no more visitors from number five.'

It was a pity, Mahmood thought afterwards, that they would not be able to be good neighbours with number five after all. They could not be on happy visiting terms with them, as he'd originally hoped.

Remembering the adoring look on Mirza's face as he gazed up at Sandra, he realised that it would be far too risky.

He believed in live and let live. He had always respected the Gorbals neighbours for being good Christians. And they had respected him for being a good Muslim. They went to their Christian church. (If they went to any church at all. Many didn't bother and so he wasn't sure what they believed.) He and his family always attended the mosque with unfailing regularity. The marriage of his dear deceased daughter and Bashir had been arranged. His daughter had never seen Bashir before the ceremony but everything had worked out well and they had been happy.

He fondly remembered that wedding day. All the men gathered in the sitting room of the Gorbals flat. All the women sat on the floor of the kitchen. His daughter was suitably veiled. The vows were taken separately, as was the custom, and then the men trooped off to the restaurant where a meal had been booked. After they returned, the women went to have their meal. At first, his daughter had gone to live with Bashir's family. Then, sadly, his daughter and Bashir's mother and father were killed and their house destroyed in a gas explosion.

As a result, it was agreed that he, Mahmood Shafaatulla, would provide a larger home so that the whole family could be together in a good area, and they moved to Waterside Way. Bashir had taken over the running of the Shafaatulla grocery business and was doing extremely well. He had lived in Glasgow all his life, of course, although not in the Gorbals. He had lived with his well-off parents in a very good area at the other side of Glasgow, but Waterside Way was just as good, Mahmood thought proudly. A very respectable place.

He still felt annoyed at Mirza. The boy should have known better. He wondered if, despite Mirza's obvious opposition to the idea, he should talk to Sandra's mother, just to let her know that he had reprimanded Mirza and reminded him that any liaison between a Muslim like him and a Christian girl like Sandra was unacceptable and impossible. Before he had a chance to make up his mind, there was some sort of trouble outside.

He ran to the front door, opened it a crack – just enough to enable him to peek anxiously from it. Poor Mrs McIvor, who had, he understood, an elderly person's illness of the mind, was shouting and violently struggling with her daughter and also with Mae Kelly outside number one.

Apparently, Mrs McIvor had become determined that the house at number one was where she lived and that her daughter had locked her out. Her daughter was a very good woman who looked after her mother, kept her at home and did not abandon her to some institution, as so many British people did with their elderly parents.

He greatly admired and respected Doris McIvor.

He saw Jack Kelly, the police husband of Mae Kelly, arrive and struggle from his car. Mahmood knew all the names, partly by overhearing conversations as he was doing now, and partly from Bashir who had had friendly conversations with the Kellys and the McIvors. Bashir knew all the gossip.

Poor Jack Kelly had been injured at the Ibrox football disaster

82

and it was obvious that he suffered great pain. Now he limped hastily towards the still violently struggling Mrs McIvor. He put an arm around her to lead her gently but firmly towards house number two. Then he went away to park his car, leaving his wife and Doris McIvor to take the old lady into the house.

Mahmood withdrew but even after he'd closed his door on his small, thin body, he could hear Mrs McIvor shouting,

'I'll get the police on you.'

He sighed. Poor Doris. What a good, patient daughter she was. He prayed to Allah that she would be rewarded in heaven. As soon as Bashir arrived home, he told him all about what he'd witnessed and heard.

His wife Rasheeda had been busy in the kitchen and had not seen or heard anything.

'Och, I know.' Bashir shook his head. 'I'm really sorry for that girl. The other day I saw her chasing after her mother down at the river's edge. She was terrified that her mother would fall into the water. I rescued the old woman on that occasion. Apparently she gets out the front door the moment Doris's back is turned. Then she's off like a shot. Doris told me it once took her so long to find her, she had to ask the police for help.'

'Well, that was the police helping her again today. The police officer, Jack Kelly, at number one. The poor man could hardly walk. I cannot understand why he is still able to keep his job.'

'They've given him a desk job, a regular day shift. So that he can still earn some money, I suppose, and also not be bored sitting at home all the time.'

'Everyone has their problems,' Mahmood said and he told Bashir about his worry with Mirza. 'I was thinking I might yet talk to Mrs Arlington-Jones. She might want to know that Mirza has been suitably reprimanded.'

'No, no, Pop,' Bashir said. 'You'd only make things worse. I'd have nothing to do with that woman. I said a polite good morning to her one day and she just about knocked me over, pushing past me without a word.'

'I cannot believe,' Mahmood said, 'how different some people are here. People were so friendly before.'

Bashir's brown face creased into a dimpled grin.

'This isn't the Gorbals, Pop. It's time you recognised that.'

22

'Do not forget the Scottish tea,' Mahmood reminded the women. The two men from number four were coming to visit. They were teachers, one of them in Mirza's school and the other in a private, boys only school, and so they were important people indeed.

A plate of cakes and a plate of biscuits were also important. It was the Glasgow custom. In the Gorbals, much cake and many biscuits were eaten. He had discovered too that minced beef and mashed potatoes and fish and chips were popular. (Oh, how often he'd longed for royal chicken and almond sauce. His wife Rasheeda had her dream too. She often spoke longingly of mango ice cream and milk balls made in syrup.)

The two men arrived and introduced themselves as Clive and Paul. Clive was the one who taught in the private school. Paul taught in the secondary school that Mirza attended. They seemed to enjoy the tea provided by the women.

After the women disappeared back into the kitchen, Mahmood said, 'I am worried about my son, Mirza. Do you know him?'

'Yes, of course,' both men answered.

'And Sandra-Arlington Jones?'

'Yes. Why?'

Mahmood shook his head sadly.

'It cannot be. It is wicked. We have always been good Muslims. It would greatly help, I have been thinking, if Mirza was in a different school. At present, you see, he is with that girl every day in the same school – your school.' One bony finger pointed at Paul. 'But if he was at your school,' the finger switched to Clive's direction, 'how much better everything would be. Your school is private and boys only, no girls allowed. That is what matters – no girls allowed.'

'In the first place,' Paul said coldly, 'the schools don't belong to us. We only work there.'

'And in the second place,' Clive interrupted, 'the school I teach in is a private Christian school. The headmaster could not allow Mirza's entrance.'

Mahmood said, 'If you recommended his application, he would. It will only be for a couple of years, then he will be at university and I will find him a good and suitable wife. Meantime he must get into your school and away from any contact with Sandra Arlington-Jones.'

'As Paul said, Mr Shafaatulla, we only work at the school.'

'You are a teacher, Mr Clive. You will have influence. Recommend Mirza and that will make all the difference to the headmaster. I beg of you, Mr Clive. I only want the best for my son. I want to protect him.'

'It will not be the best for Mirza to disrupt his education by changing schools.'

Both Clive and Paul rose. Paul said, 'Mirza is a good boy and Sandra is a nice girl. I wish them both every happiness.'

Mahmood followed them to the door with much wringing of hands and agitation.

'So do I. So do I. But not together. That can never be. My wife Rasheeda and I will find Mirza a good wife. But first of all, he must have a good education.'

Paul said, 'He is getting a good education where he is. I can assure you of that, Mr Shafaatulla. And he is a very intelligent boy. His ambition is to be an architect and if he continues his education where he is and then gets an appropriate place at university, I'm confident he will succeed.'

'Yes,' Clive agreed. 'You would definitely ruin the boy's chances if you disrupted his life by trying to change his school just now.'

'But surely . . .' Mahmood began to protest but was stopped by Paul.

'Forget it!'

'Far from recommending your application,' Clive said, 'I'd object most strongly to it.'

At the door, Mahmood shook his head. 'I do not understand. I am most surprised and I am very disappointed in you. Very disappointed indeed.'

'And we in you.'

Outside the door, Paul said, 'Could you beat that?'

Clive shook his head. 'I know my school has an excellent academic reputation but it's obviously not for that reason that he wants Mirza to go there.'

'I know, and if he did manage to get Mirza in, can you imagine how the poor lad would stick out like a sore thumb, looking and being so different from the others. He'd be picked on, for sure.'

'I don't know about that. My pupils are good lads. But you could be right. It could turn out to be a difficult situation. But just to disrupt Mirza's education by changing his school would be bad enough.'

'Poor Mirza and it's all because of his love for Sandra. Isn't life damnably unfair.'

'Let's include them in our prayers tonight, Paul.'

And they did. Down on their knees beside their bed as usual, they recited the Lord's Prayer and then they added,

'And please, Jesus, have mercy on Mirza Shafaatulla and Sandra Arlington-Jones. Please protect them from harm and help them to be happy together and to go on loving each other in peace and freedom. For this is the Kingdom, the Power and the Glory, for ever and ever, for Jesus' sake, Amen.'

The first opportunity they got, they spoke to Bashir and Bashir said, 'I know. It's absolutely damnable. I've tried over and over again to speak to Pop, but it's no use. All it's made him do is hurry his plans to find what he called "a suitable Pakistani Muslim wife" for Mirza. He can't find any in Glasgow and he's actually talking now about travelling over to Pakistan to find one.'

'Serve him right,' Paul said, 'if Mirza and Sandra got married at Gretna Green while he's away.'

'That's a thought!' Bashir said. 'And a romantic one. I wonder if they still marry couples over the anvil in the smiddy. Hundreds used to run away from England to be married there. It was the first place over the border, I think, where they could be married at sixteen – the law in Scotland – and without their parents' permission.'

'Serve the old guy right,' Paul repeated.

'Here, you might have made a serious point,' Bashir said thoughtfully. 'There would be nothing Pop could do if the young couple were legally married by the time he came back from Pakistan.'

'Have a secret word with Mirza,' Clive said, 'and see what he thinks.'

'I will.'

'And we'll help all we can,' Paul said. 'We could probably even rustle up a few bob if he needed financial help.'

'That's kind of you, boys, but money wouldn't be a problem. I've got plenty for a start, and I'll certainly help them financially, and in every way I can.'

Clive couldn't help laughing.

'I bet once you tell him about the Gretna Green idea, you'll have a job holding him back from immediately rushing away there with Sandra.'

'Oh, but I must. It wouldn't be safe otherwise. There's no telling what Pop might do to prevent Mirza running away though. He's surprisingly ruthless and obsessional about doing things the proper way and being true to their faith, as he sees it.'

Paul said, 'Mirza is a kind boy and a good Muslim. He also shows respect to other people's faiths. He has always shown respect to Clive and me, despite knowing that we are devout Christians.'

Clive patted Bashir's shoulder. 'He's like you, Bashir. We admire you for being a good Muslim and a good, kind man.'

'Thanks, pal. I'll try to speak to Pop again. Really plead with him, because I really don't want to do anything behind his back. But poor Mirza. If I'm forced to, I'll have to help him. He's in such a state.'

23

Hand in hand, Mirza and Sandra climbed the hill in the park to their usual place behind some bushes. Mirza had brought his binoculars and Sandra also had a pair. They didn't need them to see the beautiful towering university. It was near enough on the hill behind them. They gazed instead down across the sprawling park and green area, and then the familiar line of houses facing on to Waterside Way and the River Kelvin. Further away they could see the imposing Kelvingrove Art Galleries. Then there were the tenements and shops on Argyle Street, Sauchiehall Street, Dumbarton Road and a plethora of other streets reaching beyond to the River Clyde. They loved this wide view of the city to which they both felt they belonged. Eventually, they lay down on the grass. They cuddled their arms around each other and spoke of the future.

Mirza was hoping to train as an architect once he left secondary school and that wouldn't be long now.

'Think of it, Mirza,' Sandra said with wonder in her voice. 'Once you're an architect, you can design your own house.'

'I know.' Mirza sounded full to overflowing with pride and happiness at the thought. 'But not my house, *our* house.'

His hand began caressing her cheek, her neck and then

gradually slid down to cup her breast. She did not resist him and after his hand eased up her clothes, he began to explore every part of her.

Then suddenly, horrifyingly, a voice bawled out, 'You black bastard!'

Both Mirza and Sandra struggled to their feet.

A white youth was now shouting through the bushes to the other side.

'Come over here. There's a black bastard needs teaching a lesson.'

Sandra grabbed Mirza's hand.

'Come on, run.'

'I can handle myself.' Mirza resisted her frantic pulling.

'Mirza, for God's sake,' she shouted at him. 'I'll never speak to you again if you don't run. Right now. I swear it.'

So they swooped away like a couple of wild birds.

Once down the hill, Mirza gasped breathlessly, 'It's never any use running away, Sandra. It makes you look as if you're afraid – a soft mark – and I'm not.'

'I know, darling, but I saw a whole pack of them coming. It was the only sensible thing to do. And did you see who they were? Did you not recognise the uniform they were wearing? They must go to that small private school in the West End. You would have thought they'd know better.'

'You would think a Pakistani Muslim would know better but I bet there isn't a Pakistani Muslim in Glasgow (except Bashir) who wouldn't condemn me.'

Sandra sighed too. 'Now our lovely meeting place is spoiled. We'll not be able to go there again.'

'We'll find somewhere else.'

'It was so lovely there.'

'We'll find another private place somewhere – just for us.'

She nodded, smiled up at him and hugged his arm close.

'I thought you were afraid your mother would see us.'

'Oh, I'm forgetting.' Quickly she withdrew from him.

'Mirza said, 'I wish we didn't need to deceive anybody.'

'So do I, Mirza, but believe me, we've no choice. My mother would believe it such a disgrace, such a showing-up if she found out. She'd never forgive me.'

They parted just before they reached Museum Road, Mirza going to the left and Sandra to the right. For a couple of minutes, Mirza stopped to admire Sandra's slim figure and mass of long, wavy red-blonde hair as she made her way round to number five. Everyone used only their front doors because the ground at the back doors was usually a sea of mud, a rough muddy slope going down to Museum Road. After Sandra had disappeared, Mirza went round to the Waterside Way front entrances and went into number three.

'Where have you been, you wicked boy?' His father immediately pounced on him. He was always 'you wicked boy' now.

'Walking.'

'Walking where?' Mahmood's small thin frame bent nearer.

'Walking all this time after school and alone.'

'Are you lying to your father, you wicked boy?'

'Oh, for God's sake. I can't stand this. I'm away to the Galleries to meet some pals from school. Anything to get out of here.'

He banged out of the house and made his way along the river side and then the wide, well-kept path to the back entrance, rather than try to scramble up the slope facing the house.

He wasn't meeting any pals from school at the Art Galleries, or anywhere else. Although they all often used to go to the Galleries when they were young lads. But that was before he and Sandra got together. The Art Galleries had always been their magic place. It didn't dominate the landscape the way that Glasgow University did from its lofty hilltop position. It was only passers-by on Argyle Street or the park visitors who could appreciate the red granite towers encrusted with sculpture. Once you climbed the wet granite steps from the back of the Gallery or from the front, rain-lashed Argyle Street and entered through the doors into the breathtaking majesty of the central hall, you were enchanted. For the duration of your visit, the city outside ceased to exist. Inside, you were in a magic world. Even today, its magic could dissolve away Mirza's anger and resentment and all he could feel was the delight and the enchantment.

As a potential architect, he was fascinated by the splendid detail of the building. The stone details inside were crafted as exquisitely as the exterior, representing everything from great Scottish heroes and the ancient Guilds of Glasgow to famous European composers. Then there was the magnificent 602 (City of Glasgow) Squadron Spitfire in the West Court hanging from the ceiling. He guessed it must have been a very difficult job to figure out how it could be hung like that successfully without any danger of either bringing the roof down or the plane diving down and injuring visitors.

He wandered aimlessly for a time, stopping eventually to admire some pottery by an artist known to archaeologists as the Liperi Painter. In particular, he stared at a very rare ceramic calyx-krater, a vessel used for mixing wine with water. This collection was donated by Paul Stevenson, and Mirza was familiar with and fascinated by the story about Stevenson. He had bought an island and built a factory next to the island's live volcano and when it erupted on three separate occasions, Stevenson was blamed for this. They said Stevenson's Presbyterian beliefs had driven away the island's Roman Catholic priest, bringing bad luck. By this time, and before he left the island for good, Stevenson had bought the contents of twenty ancient Greek tombs. Their precious contents were donated to the Kelvingrove Art Galleries and Museum on his death. It never ceased to amaze, fascinate and delight Mirza how every part of the building, from its glorious architecture to its fabulous contents, were available for every citizen of Glasgow and the world to admire and be filled with wonder at.

He went to the portrait gallery and admired his favourite portrait because it was so like Sandra – or how she would be when she was older. It was a portrait study by JW Goddard of a beautiful woman with a mass of thick red-gold hair spilling over her back and shoulders. A gold band held up hair that curled down over her forehead.

Sandra's hair was as luxurious and beautiful as the name-less model's in the painting. But she hadn't the model's mature, calm look. Sandra had a tentative innocence in her expression. And an anxiety that often stretched into fear. If they could just keep their love affair secret until they at least got to university, they might be able to enjoy a safer and happier time. Architecture, the course he was going to take, was a very long one and so, if they waited until he was finished university and had taken his degree, and Sandra had qualified too, they would both be well into their twenties. He wondered if they could get secretly married while they were still studying. What could their parents do once they were married? They could cut off their financial help for a start and that might end their chances of staying at university. Even though they both tried to earn money by having evening or weekend jobs, it still might not be enough. Anyway, he'd heard that so many students needed and were searching for jobs, they had become hard to come by.

Briefly he thought that by the time they were studying at university, attitudes might have changed. But it was only for a second. People like the Reverend Denby and Sandra's mother and his father did not change. Not ever.

Once out of the front entrance of the Galleries, he trailed down towards Argyle Street, numbly kicking a stone along in front of him.

'Hi Mirza.'

Looking up, he saw two Pakistani lads from his class, Maq and Ali.

'Hi.'

'Where's Sandra?'

'We went out together earlier and a mob of white gits chased us. I'd needed to have been Superman to take on a crowd like that.'

'Christian gits, I bet, going to punish you for being a Muslim. And having the nerve to be with a Christian girl. That would be their excuse, anyway.'

It was always to do with religion. From his family's point of view. And Sandra's. It made him furious. He especially hated all the mumbo jumbo of religion. Not just the Muslim rules and regulations, but the Christian ones as well. The Catholics with their rituals and their priests with their fancy dresses and their unnatural celibacy vows. Where in the Bible did it say that priests had to be celibate? Then there were all the miserable Protestant sects with all their narrow-minded rules, supposedly, according to the Reverend Denby, coming from God Almighty. And what about the Buddhists with their gods? And the Hindus, to mention but a few religious beliefs? They couldn't all be right, but each of them believed they were, of course.

Religion had caused more unhappiness, more guilt, more pain, more suffering, more bloody wars, all down through history than anything else.

Why couldn't two people like he and Sandra just be allowed to love and cherish each other in peace?

He felt so much anger and resentment at the stupid unfairness of it all, he was tempted to shout from the rooftops that he loved Sandra.

He didn't want to hide their love. He wasn't ashamed of it. He felt himself teetering on the edge of open rebellion.

24

On another day, Clive and Paul had just come out of the Kelvingrove Art Galleries and were walking round the side to take a long way round. They, and any of the other residents, seldom, if ever, slid down the slope and on to the river's edge to Waterside Way. They'd enjoyed a nice tea and were looking forward to returning home. Then suddenly they heard the Reverend Denby's raucous roar.

'An abomination in the sight of the Lord. They deserve to suffer. And suffer they must.' There was a roar of agreement from the crowd who were listening to him. And suddenly all hell was let loose as the Reverend Denby pointed towards them and shouted, 'There's two of the filthy poofs. Destroy them! Stamp them out! God says man must not lie with man . . .'

Clive and Paul ran. Their first and natural instincts were to head for home and that is what they raced towards. But they were not quick enough and in a matter of seconds, they had been felled to the ground and were disintegrating in agony from kicks to the face and stomach.

Vaguely, faintly, they heard an urgent voice shout, 'Phone 999!' Someone must have done so because the next thing they knew, they were in hospital beds. They could not see each other at first because of the amount of bandages covering their faces and heads. Nor could they speak. It was agony to move their chests to breathe, far less speak.

It wasn't until days later that they were able to talk, or rather weakly whisper to Bashir and Jack Kelly when they came to visit.

Unfortunately, they couldn't tell their two friends that they would be able to identify their attackers. They thought they remembered hearing the Reverend Denby's voice but they couldn't be sure. As far as their shattered minds could recall, he was not one of their attackers.

'I bet it was that evil man at the root of this,' Bashir said. 'He should be arrested, Jack, and charged with attempted murder.'

'There's nothing I'd like better. But without any identification or definite proof, there's nothing much we can do, other than what we're trying to do at the moment.'

Even after Clive and Paul were able to leave the hospital and be taken home with Bashir in Jack's car, they still couldn't remember exactly what happened.

'All I can remember,' Paul said, 'is somebody shouting "Phone 999". And thank God they did. Otherwise we'd be dead by now.'

'Well, if anything more does come back to you, let me know immediately,' Jack said.

'Don't worry. We will.'

Jack helped both men back into house number four, before leaving to go to his own house.'

'You're a pal, Jack,' Clive called after him. 'We really appreciate your help. Don't we, Paul?'

'Yeah, definitely.'

'I'd better get back to Mae but if you need anything else, just let her know. Mae used to be a nurse and if need be, she'll look after you.'

'Thanks, pal,' both men cried out as Jack left the house.

'Thank God for Jack Kelly,' Clive said. 'And you, Bashir.'

Bashir made them both a cup of tea and before he left, he said, 'Just let me know any time you need me.'

'Thanks, pal.'

Once they were alone, Clive said, 'I must confess, Paul, my faith has gone very shaky. I mean, where was God while we were being attacked? And who else could have been at the root of such an attack but the devout Christian, the Reverend Denby. I can't remember though. Can you?'

'No, I'm still completely shattered. But like you, my faith has taken a beating.'

'Yes, what good is it, Paul? I mean, if God made us, why did he make us like this? And if God is love, how can he love us if he allows people to treat us like this?'

'Some people think that people like us make a decision as adults that we'll be gay but it's not like that. At least it wasn't like that for me. As far back as I can remember, I've felt the same.'

'It's not a matter of choice.'

'No, the choice comes in when you choose to hide the fact. So many men have done that in the past. Even got married and fathered children. They lived a lie and were miserable for years. Now it's gradually getting easier to "come out" – as they say.'

'Well, I'm glad we did anyway.'

'So am I but what are we going to do now, Paul? I'm too frightened to go outside the safety of our own front door.'

'We're still suffering from shock. We'll get over it once our bodies and minds have had time to heal properly.'

'You hope.'

'Well, we were all right for quite a while, Clive. We were enjoying ourselves.'

'The Reverend Denby has enjoyed his first real success. What do you bet he'll try for a repeat performance?'

'If we could just get our faith back, Clive. That's what made us feel strong and confident.'

'Maybe God was testing us.'

'To hell with that.'

'Now, Paul, remember how Jesus was tested. He never lost faith.'

'I've said it before and I'll say it again. We don't have his courage.'

'But we've always had faith in him.'

'I know, but you said he'll be with us always, protecting us from all evil. And he wasn't, Clive. He wasn't.'

For a while, they lapsed into miserable and helpless silence, in which the clock on the mantelpiece tic-tocked mercilessly.

They didn't know what to do or what to think any more.

Eventually, Paul said, 'Mae Kelly was a nurse. She'll know what to do. Jack said she'd look after us. We'll get better. We'll be all right.'

And as it turned out, Mae did them a big favour. She couldn't have done anything better for them. She found them a writers' club and a host of new and wonderful friends.

25

Mae wondered if she should lock herself in the house all day while Jack was out, so that the robbers would not be able to discover that some of the money had gone. But then there was shopping to do, food to buy, etc. And there was the hour that she would go next door to sit with old Mrs McIvor.

Should she keep out of the house all the time, keep well away and leave the robbers to do whatever they wanted? And what would that be? She could never figure it out. Never be quite sure. Never get her head round the alternatives. The robbers would be furious, of course, as soon as they realised that somebody had been helping themselves.

They were bound to be furious. But then what? A policeman's house of all places. They'd think about that. Bound to. And that would make them all the more enraged. Then what?

As soon as she reached the house after shopping, she got a terrible shock, but not the one she had feared.

Old Mrs McIvor was lying on the ground in front of the door of number one. Her white head was crimsoned with blood. Doris was standing weeping over her.

'Doris! What happened?'

'I've killed her.'

'Nonsense, you couldn't.'

'She's dead.'

Mae knelt down and searched for a pulse but found none. Old Mrs McIvor was dead.

'What happened?'

'I don't know. I can't remember. All I can remember is finding her lying there. And I wanted to kill her, Mae. I wanted her dead. I was going mad enough to do it. So I must have done it. I want to die now. I can't live with the knowledge that I've been so wicked. And what'll Alec say when he comes now? He'll want me dead. He'll know that I'm too wicked to live.'

Mae struggled to her feet.

'Stop talking like that, Doris. You're not wicked. You loved your mother. Come back into your house.' Mae put her arm round Doris's shoulders and led her back into house number two. 'Where's you mother's sedative tablets?'

Doris pointed towards a sideboard drawer and Mae hurried over to take out a tablet from the box inside. Then she ran into the kitchen to fetch a glass of water.

'Here, swallow this over. It'll calm you.'

'It might make me fall asleep.'

'That's fine. Hurry up. Just do it. Now sit down and relax. I'll see to everything.'

She helped Doris over to the nearest easy chair and propped cushions behind her.

'Keep this in your head, Doris. Keep repeating it. "I loved my mother and I'd never harm her." Keep repeating that, Doris, because it's the truth.'

Already Doris's eyelids were beginning to droop. And in a few minutes, Mae felt it safe to slip away.

She went out of the back door, round to her own back door, where she removed her muddy shoes. She left them outside her own back door and entered the house. The first place she went was the cupboard to see if the money she'd put there was still there. It wasn't. Her dreadful suspicions were confirmed. The robbers had come to take the money but either when they were trying to enter or when they were leaving, old Mrs McIvor had been struggling to get in and she struggled with them, all the time shouting as usual, 'I'll get the police to you.'

As a result, they'd either hit her or pushed her out of the way and she'd fallen. The blow to her head had killed her. Violently trembling now, Mae took a large suitcase and filled it with a change of clothing. Then she returned via the back door to Doris's house. Doris was sound asleep.

Dumping the case down, Mae reached for the telephone. She could hardly hold it, she was shaking so much. But she managed to dial the police station number.

As she sat in Doris's house, her distress became focused on Jack. If he hadn't been so bloody stupid about money and so selfish about inviting so many of his friends to the house to gorge themselves on expensive food every week, she would never have got into debt and she would never have needed to steal the money from under the floorboards. When she thought of all she'd suffered and how he had been the cause of her suffering, for the first time she experienced hatred against him. Then the doorbell rang, she hurried to go and open the door.

Local police officers on the doorstep explained they had been sent to the scene to ascertain information received and report back to the station on the possible death of a woman. She knew them all but realised they had to go through the normal procedures. They also explained that an ambulance would come but if the person was deceased, they would not remove the body.

'You can't go back into the house, Mae,' one of them said. 'We'll have to secure the area to preserve all the evidence. Is it OK if you stay here overnight?'

'Yes, no problem,' she replied. 'Poor Doris is in a state of collapse with shock. I've given her a sedative and I'd need to stay and look after her anyway. I'll have to phone her brother in Australia and tell him the awful news as well.'

'We thought it better if Jack didn't come home right away, but we'll be able to tell him now that you're OK and he doesn't need to worry.'

'Fine.'

After that she sat at Doris's front room window and watched the police tape being put round the front, side and back of house number one.

Soon, Jack arrived and limped breathlessly into Doris's house to grab Mae into his arms.

'My God, Mae. What happened?'

'I came back from Marks & Spencer and found Mrs McIvor lying dead on our doorstep.'

It was all his fault, she thought. His stupidity, his thoughtlessness, his selfishness had forced her into a morass of desperation and agonising suffering. She'd tried to tell him, tried to make him see sense, but he'd always refused to listen. She remembered with much bitterness the last time she'd desperately tried to tell him the true situation, but as usual, he'd refused to listen. She remembered how he'd silenced her. He'd laughed and said, 'Where's my dinner then? My nice big juicy steak?'

Now he said, 'There's no use sitting there, Mae. The forensic team will be notified and the police photographer and the police surgeon will soon be there. Everything's under control. Did you bring your shopping in here? We might as well relax and have something to eat.'

'A nice big juicy steak?'

He was obviously unaware of the heavy sarcasm in her tone because he said, 'Great,' and happily rubbed his hands together. 'We'll have plenty of time to enjoy our meal before the CID guys come round all the houses making their enquiries.'

God, she thought, still in a state of collapse at the awful turn of events. How had she ever managed to put up with him for so long?

26

Jack said to Mae, 'By the way, I told Clive and Paul that they'd be OK. If they ever needed to be looked after, you'd look after them.'

Wasn't that typical, she thought. In between nursing Doris, he expected her to be able to nurse two men as well. And at any moment, he'd be announcing that all his police pals would be arriving for their usual Sunday dinner.

'By the way, we'll be able to get back to our own place tomorrow.'

They had been staying in Doris's house until their own place was cleared by the police. By this time, Alec McIvor had arrived and, seeing the helpless state his sister was in (Mae had continued to administer sedatives), he asked Mae if she would be Doris's carer.

'I'll arrange through our solicitors for you to be paid a regular wage, Mae, and a very generous one, if you'd please take on the job. It would put my mind at rest if you'd agree.'

She agreed.

'Well,' Jack said, 'make sure you make it clear that you'll be doing it part time.'

'Why?' she asked. 'What do you mean?' knowing exactly what he meant. He meant that she had to be available to make his 'juicy steak' dinners every night and have all the necessary Marks & Spencer meals ready for his mob of police pals every Sunday.

'You're a married woman, Mae. Your first duty is to your husband.'

'Well, I'm sorry, Jack, but I've taken on this commitment and I must honour it. Poor Doris is definitely needing me to nurse her back to health.'

Jack rolled his eyes. 'Well, I hope she'll recover soon. Meantime, we'll gather our things together ready to move back to our own place tomorrow.'

'You can gather your things, Jack. I'm staying here to nurse Doris full time. I must be available during the night as well as during the day.'

'You can't do that.'

'Yes, I can.'

'But who'll cook dinner every day? Especially dinner on Sundays.'

'I'm afraid you'll have to cook them yourself meantime, Jack, and do the shopping for all your nice, juicy steaks.' Again, her little sarcasm passed unnoticed by him.

He was obviously furious.

'Well, don't expect me to pay you your housekeeping money, as well as pay for all the food myself,' he shouted indignantly.

'I'm not expecting that, Jack. By all means, use the house-keeping money to buy your steaks and fish suppers, and puddings and whatever else you fancy from Marks & Spencer.'

He really believed that the paltry few pounds he gave her would buy all the food he and his pals happily gorged on. Oh, just wait, she thought. What a surprise he was about to receive. Shock, more like. She could hardly wait to see the result of his foray into Marks & Spencer.

Meantime, she enjoyed the rest she was having in Doris McIvor's house. It was a rest because she and Doris got on well together and Doris wasn't in the least demanding. She slept most of the time and when she wasn't asleep, they enjoyed a light meal together while watching television. Doris had a packed freezer and fridge and so she didn't even have to go out shopping.

'My brother was over, wasn't he? Or have I been imagining seeing Alec?' Doris asked occasionally. She was forgetful and repetitive, but not nearly as bad as her mother had been.

'No, dear. Your brother was over and he really cares about you. He's asked me to stay with you and look after you. He's even arranged for me to be paid a good wage as your nurse and carer. Which is very nice for me.'

'Very nice for me too, Mae. I feel so much safer and better now that you're with me all the time.'

After a minute or two, she said, 'Tell me again that I didn't kill my mother, Mae.'

'You didn't kill your mother, Doris. I saw two men hanging about. I told the police when they were questioning everybody. They knew the men. They've been after them for a robbery at the Art Galleries.'

'I wonder why . . .'

'Doris, you know how your mother kept shouting, "I'll get the police on you"?'

'Oh yes, poor soul. I forgot about that.'

'I've no doubt she shouted it at these two criminals, and they killed her to silence her.'

Gradually Doris relaxed.

At last she said, 'My poor mother. You're right, of course. That must be what happened. It's just I got such a shock. I'd been under so much stress for so long and . . .'

'I know. I know. But now you must relax and get better, Doris.'

'Please don't leave me, Mae.'

'I'm not going to leave you, Doris. I'm very happy staying

here with you. I enjoy your company and it's a lovely wee job for me.'

It was the truth. She felt happy and relaxed.

She felt upset though when she thought of what had happened to poor Clive and Paul from house number four. She popped in to see them and was shocked at their appearance. They had black eyes and broken noses and scars on their cheeks.

'I'm so sorry about what happened to you. What a disgrace that people can behave like that – like wild animals. I can't do much to help you, I'm afraid, because I'm nursing Doris. Her brother is paying me to be her full time nurse and carer.'

'That's all right, Mae. We'll manage. Bashir has been filling our fridge and we're able to walk about the house now and cook our meals. Not that we're able to eat much yet.'

'Well, I'm glad you're on the mend. I'll pop in again as soon as I can.'

'Thanks, Mae.'

They struggled to their feet and Mae said, 'I'll see myself out. Just you relax where you are.'

'The only thing is,' Clive said, 'we're both terrified to show our faces outside our door now. God knows when we'll ever have the courage to go out again.'

Paul sighed.

'Before this, we enjoyed our visits to the Art Galleries so much.'

'You'll soon get your courage back,' Mae assured them. 'And the first time you go out, Jack and Bashir will go with you. Don't worry about it. Just give your physical wounds time to heal first.'

'We're lucky we've got such good friends,' Paul said. 'The writers from the club are coming to visit us too. We're looking forward to that.'

'Good.' Mae gave them a wave. 'Have a great time.'

27

Clive and Paul had become members of a writers' club and the club was having a night for members at their house, reading samples of their work out loud. Clive listened with great pride as Paul read:

Learning to Listen

The wind pulled voices
across my window
with the insistence
of chalk across the blackboard,
like high squeals of warning
from a loose-hinged gate.

Here on a bridge girded by secrets
the same voices whisper snippets
from dark, shallow grooves in the stone.
They slide words at me across the brick
like pebbles sent skimming over a river
hard-edged with gossip.

Some I manage to evade, others
strike home with the cutting flint of truth,
once I recognise the curve of your speech.

I should learn to listen,
allow the words to settle
in that padded-room
between denial and understanding.

It would be easier to place one foot
on the low wall of the bridge
spread my arms crucifix wide
lean forward
and will flight into the span of my arms.

There was enthusiastic applause and one member said,
'Here, Paul, that was good. And it's damned difficult to write
poetry. I know. I've tried. Have you got another one there?'
'Yes.'
'OK, let's hear it and then after a wee bit of discussion,
we'll go on to someone else.'

A Close Shave

It sat on the window sill
above the sink, bounced back
my father's movements as he shaved.

I would sit on my hands
on the toilet seat and watch
mouth open,
the ritual of soap and razor.

Skin was prepared,
soaked with water
hot enough to open pores,
relax wire follicles.

Bristles whisked the soap
until cream peaked.
I loved the sound of the blade
As it rasped over his face.

Breath on hold,
I watched a thin river of red
wash through white soap.
No cry of pain.
He was tough, my Dad.

Clive joined the others in clapping enthusiastically. It was such a blessing that they'd found the writers' club. There was no discrimination, no prejudice here. They had remarked on it and another member had said,

'Right enough. When you think of it, in what other profession would people help each other so much and be genuinely delighted and happy when one of them achieved success?'

Sometimes there was a speaker but always, after the formal part of the meeting, everyone enjoyed a cup of tea and a chat, or a blether to use one of Clive's favourite Scottish words. They were each given a programme when they joined and it contained an interesting mix of speakers. Some were very successful writers in different genres – playwrights, romantic authors, thriller writers, science fiction authors. They came to help by telling of how they succeeded. They also handed out typed sheets of helpful hints and suggestions. On other occasions there were speakers whose knowledge helped with research. A librarian from the Mitchell Library was listed and both Clive and Paul were looking forward to hearing him. The Mitchell Library was one of their favourite places. It had been founded by a Glasgow tobacco baron, Stephen Mitchell, and was the largest public reference library in Europe. Both Clive and Paul were great fans of the poet Robert Burns and the Mitchell had the largest collection of first editions of the poet's work, as well as a host of Burnsania. It had more than four thousand first editions in thirty two languages. The place itself was impressive. The solid Edwardian baroque building was topped by a beautiful copper dome. The Mitchell was one of many buildings in Glasgow that inspired the architecture enthusiast and poet laureate John Betjeman, to describe Glasgow as the 'greatest Victorian city in Europe'.

The writers' club was situated in Ashton Lane, off Byres Road in the West End. It was a really trendy area, with a variety of restaurants and pubs where crowds of people (mostly young people who looked like university students) stood drinking their pints outside. Further along, there were a few tables and chairs in front of a small restaurant. When Clive and Paul were able to go out and about, they favoured a larger restaurant called the Ubiquitous Chip. There the food was, in their opinion, about the best in Glasgow. Many famous people ate there.

The whole atmosphere in Ashton Lane and the West End, in Clive and Paul's opinion, was very typically Glasgow. One New Yorker said that Glasgow had the disputatious cheek and the pace of Manhattan. Glasgow had grit to it and an exhilaration that made the place buzz.

Especially in the centre of the city in front of the Royal Exchange building. There, a statue of the Duke of Wellington mounted on his horse sat high on a plinth. One guide to Glasgow claimed that if Edinburgh had poise, Glasgow had swagger. And it had a determination to break free of its background of poverty and deprivation and give everything a whirl.

Clive was now having his hair done in the latest style. It was gelled up into straight peaks.

'I liked you better with it natural and smooth,' Paul told him. He had insisted on keeping his own dark hair long until it kept sliding forward over one eye.

'I see by the programme,' Paul said now, 'that there's going to be a police officer as one of the speakers. That'll be interesting to all of us, but especially to crime and thriller writers. I was just wondering if it might be Jack Kelly from number one.'

'I wouldn't think so. It would be too much of a coincidence.'

'Oh, I don't know. Remember he told us he works constant day shift so at least he'd always be free to come to an evening meeting.'

'Look, there's the name of the speaker in the programme. It's Sergeant Paul Rogers.'

'Oh well,' said Paul.

'I'm really looking forward to next week's subject. How all art can be therapeutic,' Clive quoted from the programme.

'Yeah. So am I. It's a real godsend, this place. I hope you don't mind always coming with me, Clive. I mean, writing is my thing, not yours.'

'Haven't I just said I'm really looking forward to next week? And anyway, I'm a teacher and I have to teach my class essay writing, etc. No, don't you worry about me joining the writers' club, Paul. The writers are a great bunch and I'm loving it.'

'One of the great things about writers,' Paul said, 'and about being a writer is everything is your raw material – people, experiences, places, but especially people. Even an elderly person who's not doing anything or saying anything. Remember that one I wrote called 'Disposable People'?'

'Who could forget that.'

As they stood together in the writers' club sipping their cups of tea, Paul began to quietly recite it.

Disposable People

Blind stares from milk and water
coloured eyes, reveal all
to those who would care to look.

There, the disposed sit the long day
doing nothing
saying nothing
eating bland and little,
leaching all of their nourishment
from the cathode ray nipple
housed in the black box.

A second childhood they say

A second childhood without
the toys
the joys
the expectations.

'Paul, you are so very talented but it's novels you should be concentrating on now. That's where your big successes will be. It's novels that'll make you famous.'

'I must confess that's really where my heart lies. And I'm looking forward to getting good practical help from some of the successful novelist speakers here. You see, you can say so much more about the human condition through the medium of a novel. And bring places to life, as well as people.'

'Yes, and the two you've already written are good, Paul, and maybe the speakers or other members of the club will give you a helpful crit, some advice to help you get them published.'

Paul nodded. 'Wouldn't that be wonderful. Meantime, I'll keep my hand in the writing mould with my poetry. It gives me something to take to the club every week. And keeps me being creative and happy. Nothing our awful neighbours can do will ever spoil that.'

28

Paul was reading his new poems at the writers' club, eager for feedback.

For Worse

Coloured grey,
gilded with sweat,
large enough to grind
flour for the world's poor,
granite hangs around her neck

Every movement
she sees the man
and forgets
the child.

She waits the thrill of the phone
someone else's life.
She dreams of better times,
resents the vow that doesn't list
what 'for worse' might entail.

But she can forget the wife
and be the woman

for a rosary of moments,
It might save them both.

Afternoon Tea and Teeth

It was the sort of tearoom where ladies would attend
an anecdote, the curve at either end of their
smile as thin as a crochet hook, while they promised
themselves they would laugh later.

One such lady of lavender years
sat at the far end of the hush, silver-lipped, lilac twin-set,
lean as a walking cane, face creased in crepe as she rued
the young women of the day and their
penchant for coffee with foamed milk
and their *insistence* on a career.

Maybe it was the child behind her
fitted snugly at her mother's naked breast,
or that woman's vulgar handbag
gold lettering against white, screaming DIOR
. . . but something made her sneeze.

Her head moved in increments
ratcheted back by her desperate desire
not to draw attention, but the tickle insisted.
The pressure built, her head jerked forward
and her teeth bulleted out of her mouth,
complete with a lady's bite-sized portion
of date and wholemeal scone.

Face polished white with resolve not to be noticed
she slid off her chair and on hands and knees
crawled across the room, retrieved her dentures
and popped them in her mouth, complete with scone.
Remaining low she returned to her seat
and a more considered chewing action.

Not a stitch in the room's conversation
was dropped. In a concert of collusion not one eye
strayed during the retrieval, invisibility
guaranteed by the collective will to do
and say the right thing.

Another lady paused
at her friend's no doubt embroidered comments,
pushed her tongue against the roof of her mouth
and harrumphed into a square of bleached linen.
Just in case.

'All right,' Clive told Paul. 'They're good.' Everyone in the
writers' club agreed the poems were good but they also agreed
that Paul should be concentrating on writing a novel – a
publishable novel. The two he had written had been passed
around and given verbal and written crits. The books (like
many of his poems) were written from a woman's viewpoint.

'I believe that's where you're going wrong, certainly in the
novels,' Sheena Brown said. 'You keep insisting that novels
are your first love and you're desperate to get one published
but I don't think you'll ever succeed until you start writing
from a man's viewpoint.'

'OK,' Ray Cook said, 'we know you're gay. So why don't
you write from a gay man's viewpoint?'

'I keep telling him that,' Clive cried out, 'but he won't listen
to me.'

Paul cast his eyes heavenwards. 'No wonder. You of all people know what we have to suffer from a lot of people. I don't need publishers joining in.'

'But, wait a minute,' Ray said. 'I'm sure publishers wouldn't be prejudiced like that. There's bound to be publishing firms that publish gay material. Look up the *Writers and Artists Yearbook*. That's probably where I've come across them.'

'Gay publishing firms?' Paul echoed incredulously.

'Yes, why not? Give it a try,' Ray insisted. 'Put all your feelings into a novel about what gay men have to suffer.'

'Gosh,' Clive laughed, 'think of the revenge you could have – on people like that ghastly reverend gentleman at number seven.' He turned to the others. 'He's a hook-nosed skeleton of a man who tells us we're an abomination in the sight of God.'

Paul visibly brightened at that. His eyes acquired a mischievous sparkle. 'Right enough, I could make a great villain of him.'

'He *is* a villain,' Clive told him, and then to the others, 'Fancy him being a minister and he shouts horrible names at us and tramples over our nice garden and kills our flowers and puts all sorts of filthy things through our letter box.'

'No!' their fellow members gasped. 'And he's supposed to have been a Christian minister?'

Maisie Jenner said, 'You should report him to the police. That's harassment.'

'All we want is to have a peaceful life,' Paul said, but brightened again. 'But do you know, you've really got me excited now. I really believe I could write a story about how people like him make people like Clive and me suffer. We'll get a *Writers and Artists Yearbook* right away and check the addresses of publishers who accept gay material.'

They had a great laugh during the tea break and exchanged all sorts of ideas about how Paul could wreak vengeance on the Reverend Denby.

'Look,' Ray said eventually, 'if you like, you can come home with me tonight and I'll give you my *Writers and Artists Yearbook*. You can return it as soon as you can.'

'We could check it in your house, if you didn't mind. Then we wouldn't need to take it away.'

'Sure. Come on. I've the car outside. We won't take a minute.'

Off they went and sure enough, in the *Writers and Artists Yearbook*, they found several who specifically published gay material. Paul was over the moon.

'Oh, thanks a million, Ray. I'll never be able to thank you enough.'

'You can thank me by presenting me with a signed copy of your first published novel.'

'Deal!' He and Paul smacked hands together. Then Ray drove them home.

After they got into number four Waterside Way, Paul said, 'Talk about a friend in need being a friend indeed. What a good friend that is.'

'Yes,' Clive agreed. 'But of course they know that we'd always do the same for any of them when they need help. Already you've helped a couple of them to write poetry, Paul. In fact, you've done quite a few helpful crits for the members who want to be poets.'

'Right enough. But now I must organise my time so that I can get down to writing my novel right away. Do you know, I think I'm going to enjoy doing this one. The characters will be set in a different place, of course, and will look different, etc.'

'Even in real life,' Clive said, 'I bet Denby is not the good Christian gentleman these two posh characters believe he is.'

Paul looked thoughtful. 'I wonder if our pal Bashir knows more about him and those two women. Bashir's a great one for the gossip about everybody.'

'I don't think he'll have succeeded with the two women.

Remember he said he got a right brush off from them. And he, like us, was just trying to be friendly.'

'I could always ask him anyway.'

A time schedule for his writing was arranged, with Paul getting up at six o'clock in the morning to write for a couple of hours before breakfast and setting out for his work at the school.

Before long, he was happily wreaking his revenge on not only the Reverend Denby, but on the double-barrelled character and Mrs Jean Gardner as well.

29

Clive and Paul strolled through the galleries, admiring the latest exhibition.

'Certainly original,' Paul said. 'I've never seen the like of it in my life – anywhere. Have you?'

Clive shook his head. 'It's a really wonderful and original place all together. They call the Kelvingrove Art Gallery and Museum a portal to the world, and rightly so.'

'I was glad the Reverend Denby didn't get a sympathetic audience when he was giving his ridiculous sermon in the park. Fancy condemning such a beautiful place as evil. I suppose he was thinking of all the pictures and sculptures of naked women. Anyway he won't be able to do it now.'

'Surely he hasn't really been inside,' Clive said. 'The paintings are so beautiful. One of my favourite things is actually a sculpture. That heart-rending plaster called *Motherless* – the one with the child in the arms of a distraught father. But everyone, even the Reverend Denby, must sure admire and be moved by Salvador Dali's *Christ of St John of the Cross*.'

'Not nutters like the Reverend Denby. Probably it was him that attacked it.'

'God, yes.' Clive rolled his eyes. 'I forgot about that. It was attacked twice. Once the canvas was punctured with a sharp stone and then ripped open. The other time it was attacked with an air gun.'

'I'll never be able to understand the thinking behind that,' Paul said, 'and as a writer, I'm supposed to understand what makes all sorts of people tick. What motivates them. I keep trying to work out how the Reverend Denby can believe he's a Christian. What Jesus is he acting on behalf of?'

'It's the Old Testament he keeps quoting and raving on about.'

'I know, but he claims to be a Christian and a Christian is supposed to be a follower of Jesus Christ.'

'Och, let's try to forget about that nutter and enjoy the Gallery.' Clive liked the painting *Old Willie – The Village Worthy* by Paul Guthrie. Paul admired Cadell's masterpiece *Interior – The Orange Blind*.

'That orange blind in the background,' he said, 'provides the picture with a dazzling focal point and contrasts so starkly with the bold expanses of black and green. And of course, we're left with the puzzle of who is the man in the background playing the piano and who is the mysterious lady in the foreground taking tea. The whole thing has a sense of nervous energy and expectation.'

'It's a bit like *Lady with a Red Hat* in a way,' Clive said, going over to stare at the portrait by William Strang. 'The bold colours and elegant posture make it, for me, one of the most striking portraits in the collection.'

'It's Vita Sackville West,' Paul said, 'aristocratic poet, novelist and lesbian. Her lesbian affair with Virginia Woolf was immortalised in Woolf's novel *Orlando*.'

'Yes, I read that years ago. I remember reading about the stir it made at the time. And just you wait and see, Paul. Your book about gay men will make just as big a stir.'

'It's not written yet, Clive.'

'Not finished yet, but you're getting there, Paul. It's

wonderful that you've been able to do so much as you have, when you're working at teaching full time.'

Neither of them were all that keen on Lowry's busy pictures of matchstick men but both stopped to admire Avril Paton's *Windows in the West*. They had both lived in tenements in the past and could relate to the glowing interior of the tenement with glimpses of people going about their everyday lives inside.

It was while they stood admiring *Windows in the West* that they noticed a young couple walking nearby. Clive nudged Paul.

'That's Mirza Shafaatulla and Sandra Arlington-Jones, isn't it?'

'Yeah. If that horrible snob of a woman saw her daughter just now, she'd have a fit. Sandra looks really besotted with Mirza, doesn't she. And he with her.'

'Real love birds, they look. Poor things. They don't stand a chance.'

Mirza and Sandra were walking along with arms entwined around each other and Sandra's head with its thick cap of red gold hair was resting against Mirza's shoulder.

Suddenly, the young people stiffened with shock and fear as they stared over at Clive and Paul.

'Don't worry,' Clive called over, but quietly, 'your secret is perfectly safe with us.'

'Thanks,' both of them mouthed in reply.

Clive and Paul moved away to study some sculpture but as they did so, Clive murmured, 'God help them' and Paul said, 'They'll need plenty of help. Mirza's Muslim parents will be against them and Mrs Arlington-Jones would, I bet, rather see Sandra dead that hitched up with Mirza.'

Suddenly Clive laughed. 'Look at that. If the Reverend Denby has been in and seen that, no wonder he's been preaching hell and damnation outside.'

'What's it called?' Paul stared at the sculpture of the naked woman.

'*Syrinx*. It's by William McMillan. One lady visitor apparently stripped off and was photographed beside it by her companion. I don't know if it was a lady companion or not. Even more interesting is Rodin's *Age of Bronze*. It had its penis stroked by so many visitors, especially lady visitors, that the bronze patina wore off. It's been restored to its originally glory and it's now at the Burrell Collection.'

Paul said, 'The reverend gentleman would definitely be horrified at that. I can just see his dashing straight from the gallery to the park and roaring out his sermon denouncing all the evils he'd just seen and heard about in here.'

Clive suddenly remembered about Mirza and Sandra. 'I hope he doesn't come across the young love birds. He'd immediately report them to Mrs Arlington-Jones. Then all hell would be let loose.'

'It's pathetic, isn't it? Why can't people live and let live. They're not doing anyone any harm by loving each other. It's the same with us.'

Clive said, 'We've had to live with unfair attitudes for a long time. But at least we're mature adults. We've had time to harden ourselves to protect ourselves from it. They're only children. Their hurt and suffering will be so much worse.'

'I know. God, talk about suffering. Look at that sculpture.' Paul pointed over at Pierre Bracke's *Wives of Fishermen*. It was a sculpture in dull grey marble of four tragic-looking women clinging close together, waiting anxiously for the return of their husbands from a storm at sea, hope fading.

'That just shows that artists don't always choose physical beauty when searching for a subject. A painful or difficult side of life can result in a more moving work of art. That's what I'm trying to do, I suppose. There's much in my book that's painful and difficult but I'm hoping the end result will be a work of art that will touch everyone.'

'And I'm sure it will be, Paul. If only you could afford to give up teaching and concentrate on writing it. You know what my wages are – not enough to keep both of us. Otherwise I'd gladly support you.'

'I wouldn't want you to be worried like that. No, I'll just carry on the way I'm doing. At least I'm happy with what I've managed to write.'

'What's bothering me, Paul, is the fact that you haven't made him a minister – the Denby character, I mean. Why are you making him a two-faced bully of a husband in the book?'

'It's the emotional truth that matters, Clive. Our writer friends would agree about that, I'm sure. It's the same with the gay characters in the book. They're not teachers like us. They don't live in a place like Waterside Way. But their suffering is true to life – our life – and that's what matters.'

'I suppose you know best. You're the writer, not me. It's certainly proving to be a gripping read anyway. Oh look, there's Bashir.' Clive waved at their Muslim friend who seemed somewhat agitated.

'I've just seen the two old biddies walking towards the Gallery and I know Sandra and Mirza are there. I wanted to warn them in case they came out and bumped into the pair of old horrors.'

'We saw them just a few minutes ago.'

'Where?'

Paul pointed. 'Over there.'

'Thanks, pal. See you.'

'Aye. OK.'

After Bashir had raced away, Clive said, 'He's a really good guy, isn't he?'

'Yeah. If only everybody was like him. OK, he's Muslim, not Christian like us. But he's a good Muslim and it's how

127

people treat one another that matters. He treats people in a caring and loving way. What could be better than that?'

'You're right. I'd rather have him than the Christian Reverend Denby any day.

30

Jack Kelly said, 'I haven't even had time to do the shopping, what with all the extra work at the station.'

Mae shrugged. 'You'll have more time from now on, won't you?'

'No, I won't.' Jack's voice hardened angrily. 'You'll have to do the shopping. *And* come in and cook the meals.'

'I've told you, Jack. I must stay here with Doris.'

'And I'm telling you, you must come back to where you belong.'

'You can't tell me what to do.'

'I *am* telling you. And if necessary, I'll tell Doris as well. From now on, you're only going to work part time seeing to her.'

'Doris is ill and needing taken care of. You're perfectly strong and healthy.'

'You can take care of her part time after you do the shopping and while I'm at work. Once I'm at home, your duty is to come home and see to my meals.'

'And those of all your police friends?'

'Yes. It all worked out perfectly happily before.'

'Perfectly happily?'

'Yes. And there's no reason why it should not work out perfectly happily again.'

'Jack, how many times must I repeat myself? Doris is ill and needs to be taken care of day and night, and that is what I'm being paid to do.'

'You're forgetting something, Mae.'

'What?'

'I'm not in fact as perfectly strong and healthy as you've just said. I have an injured hip and I confess now, although you must have seen it with your own eyes, that I suffer constant agonising pain.'

She couldn't deny this and for the first time, she wavered. She might have tried to make whatever concession she could but seeing her hesitate and waiver, he immediately became aggressive again.

'So stop all this bloody nonsense, pack up your things and come home. *Now!*' he shouted at her, 'before I completely lose patience with you.'

Wasn't that so typical of him. He was a stupid, selfish bully and always had been. He'd never change. All right, she missed his passionate love-making. There was no denying he was good at sex but that couldn't, and shouldn't, make up for all his faults, and all the other things he was totally ignorant about.

'No,' she said, in the nearest to shouting she'd ever managed in her life. 'I will not pack up my things and come home. Forget it. From now on, you'll have to manage on your own.'

'Don't you dare talk to me like that.'

'I'll talk to you any way I like.'

'Did you not hear me?' His voice and facial expression turned incredulous.

'Yes, I heard you. You were shouting loud enough. It's a good job Doris has had her sedative or she would have heard you as well.'

'You will *not* talk to me any way you like. You will show me some respect, do you hear me? You'll behave at least like a half-decent wife. That means you shut up now and do as you're told.'

She nearly laughed. It was so ridiculous.

'Oh, Jack!'

'Oh Jack what?'

Did he expect her now to go down on her knees and apologise to him?

'You're being ridiculous.'

'What?' he yelled. '*I'm* being ridiculous?'

'Yes. Almost Victorian. In case you haven't noticed, women are free now, Jack. They are not slaves to their husbands.'

'The bloody trouble with you is, you don't know how lucky you are.'

'Oh yes?'

'Yes. I've provided you with a lovely home. Never kept you short of money . . .'

She nearly gave a howl of hilarity at that.

'Never been unfaithful to you. Don't even smoke or drink. What more could any woman want?'

'I want you to try doing what you expected me to do.'

'What the hell are you talking about now?'

'Do the shopping for a start, Jack. That'll be an eye opener for you. Come back and speak to me again after you do that.'

'You're raving, woman. What's so difficult about shopping? If that's all you've had to worry you, you really have been lucky.'

'That's what you've always thought, despite what I tried to tell you over and over again. I've tried to tell you the truth, Jack, but you've always refused to listen. I'm sick of telling you. I'm sick of talking to you. Just go away.'

'Maybe you'd rather have action than talk. Maybe that's what you need.'

And with that he grabbed her and dragged her across the room, his fingers digging painfully into her arms.

'You're coming home right now.'

'Let go of me, or I'll scream the place down until every house in Waterside Way hears me. I'll report you to police headquarters. What will all your precious police pals think of you then?'

He loosened his grip.

31

Mae felt sad. Jack, for all his faults, had never been a violent man. He had always been kind and helpful to everyone. And of course he'd always thought he was kind and helpful to her. Despite the constant agony he suffered, he never complained or allowed the pain to keep him from going to any lengths to help neighbours or friends. Normally he was a patient man too. He had never lost his temper in the past. Was it her fault that he had changed to much? She struggled to be fair.

Right from the start, should she have refused to buy all the equipment and furniture for the new house in Waterside Way? She had used up her savings. After that, should she have stopped, even if it meant moving in to bare floor boards, curtainless windows and empty rooms? She had wanted to please Jack, of course, but that should not have been used as an excuse to go to a wholesale warehouse and order every-thing the house needed to make it look first class. How on earth had she imagined at the time that she'd ever be able to pay the bill for all that?

The money under the floor boards had obviously proved too much of a temptation for her in the circumstances.

She had thought at the time that it had been put there by some previous eccentric tenant who had since died. It was sheer bad luck that it was money stolen from the Art Galleries.

But she should never have touched it. She had only herself to blame for that. She couldn't blame Jack. It was only natural too that he wanted to show his lovely new home to all his police officer friends. She should not have gone along with buying expensive food for them, however. She should have stood her ground and refused.

Things had just gone from bad to worse after that. Now she felt sad – sad that she had been at the root of changing Jack so much. Changing herself too. There were times when emotion got the better of her and she could even feel hatred for him. But in quiet moments she realised that fuelling the hatred were her feelings of frustration, regret and guilt.

Deep down, she still loved him. She tried not to face that, or she tried to tell herself that it was purely sexual and she'd get over it. No, all of his life, Jack Kelly had been an honest, kind-hearted, courageous man. She had loved him for it and she loved him still.

He had changed but it was her fault that he had changed. She had to face up to that unpalatable fact.

32

Jack had come apparently just for a cup of tea and a gossip about his work. Mae knew differently of course. Looking at him, she could understand what she'd always seen in him and how he'd always got round her in the past. His dark eyes had a sexual glimmer in them when he spoke to her. He was the most handsome man she'd ever known, with his sleek black hair, his strong cleft chin and broad, muscly shoulders.

'So the lads took the two neds round and in through the back door. The reception desk where I work is for members of the public coming in.' He took another sip of tea while his eyes glimmered at her over the tea cup. 'If it's a suspect or an accused, they get taken in through the back door to the charge bar. The lads had a good laugh in private afterwards. It was such a stroke of bad luck for the neds that they stashed the stolen money in a police officer's house.' He laughed, remembering. 'They didn't know at the time, of course. It was before we moved in.'

Mae said to Doris, 'Would you like some more tea, dear?'

'No thanks, Mae. I'll just go over and look out of the window. I like to see the flowers in our wee garden.'

'Will you manage all right?'

'Fine. Fine.'

Jack watched Doris move away and then said, 'She's an awful lot better, isn't she?'

'Yes, I'm glad to say.'

'I saw you walking her round to the Art Galleries the other day.'

'Yes, she really enjoyed that. She had a rest in the tea room for a while, but she managed to see a couple of the exhibits.'

'She'll soon be completely back to normal.'

'Physically, perhaps. But the years of stress she had to suffer have affected her mentally.'

'Oh, I'm sure she'll get over that too. She sounds quite sensible to me.'

Any minute now, Mae thought, he's going to get round to the true reason for his visit. And sure enough, it came.

'But for now, you'll at least be able to get out with her to do the shopping.'

'Yes, we do manage once a week. As well as hanging on to me, Doris sometimes uses a stick. Or she supports herself with the trolley I push. We use it to carry the shopping back home.'

'No problem shopping then?'

'We manage.'

'So you could quite easily pop into the trolley the steaks, etc, I need for my dinners and the Sunday dinner for my pals.'

There it was, at last. The true reason.

'But I'm not going to, Jack.'

His eyes hardened with anger. 'What do you mean, you're not going to?'

'I've told you before that I want you to do the shopping. It'll be a learning experience for you. Come back and tell me what you think afterwards.'

'What's to learn about shopping? And you've done it so often before, Mae.'

'Oh yes. So often.'

'You know the price of everything.'

'Oh yes, indeed I do.'

'Well then.'

'Jack, I tried and tried to tell you about the shopping and the price of everything and you would never listen.'

'Of course I listened. I gave you a raise in your housekeeping money. But don't think that I'm going to give you any more. You're getting no housekeeping money from me until you come back and do the housekeeping. Meantime,' he commanded, 'do the shopping!'

'I don't want any housekeeping money from you any more. I'm well paid for the job I do here.'

'This is ridiculous. You're my wife. Your first duty is to me.'

'You've a lot to learn, Jack, and your first lesson will be when you do the shopping for all the steaks and fish suppers for your Sunday dinner.'

'Are you jealous of my police friends coming to visit me? Is that your problem?'

She could have laughed but instead she just shook her head.

'No, that's not my problem, Jack. Now, if you've finished your tea, I'd like you to leave.'

He got up, nearly knocking the chair over.

'Right, I'll do the bloody shopping but I'll be back.'

'Yes, Jack, I do believe you will.'

33

Paul hadn't got very far with his novel yet but he had a poem ready to show the crowd of writers who came to have a meeting in house number four.

It was called 'Wounded Knee' and he read it to them when it was his turn to contribute something to the meeting.

Wounded Knee

My black trousers stumbled to a point half way
to the skull-grey cap of my knee
while I steered my way through the corrals
of school playtime, avoiding the gunslinger
glare of bullies, who'd queue
to lassoo with threats.

Pencil point stabbed between my shoulders,
Beef-jerky breath in my face
And a low growl in my ear . . .
. . . as soon as the bell rings, you're dead.

I was faster than any of them
knees and fists pumping the air,

I was the best rider
the Pony Express never had.
A half-breed scout, I wore
a Colt pistol under my belt
and an eagle's tail feather in my hair.

A fall . . . and the bony plate of my knee
became a wound with hard baked gravel
ground under the torn and grieving skin.

I grew my thumbnail especially
for that moment when the scab was ripe,
when the blood had hardened
to a brown as deep as the colour of apache skin.

I would tease off the scab . . .
. . . until baby pink skin winked in the sunlight,
fresh for the next gallop across the prairie
and the race into the unreachable horizon.

'Where did you get the idea for that one?' Eric Summers asked. 'Were you bullied at school because you were gay?'

'I don't know if it was because I was gay but I was certainly bullied.'

'Were you bullied as well where you were young, Clive?' Pat Jenners asked.

'Yes, I used to be terrified to go to school. Unfortunately I hadn't the release of being able to write poetry. I suppose it was a release, Paul, to express your feelings like that.'

'Yeah, definitely. I didn't have a clue then about how to write a novel, but I was a great reader and always dreamed of writing books like the ones I read and enjoyed.'

'Don't worry,' Eric said. 'You'll soon be able to get back to working on your novel. It's got such potential, Paul. We've all been enjoying what you've read to us so far.'

'Here,' Pat cried out. 'How about sending the first three chapters out to a publisher. Or to half a dozen publishers. Multiple submissions are allowed now.'

'I know,' Paul said, 'but in the *Writers and Artists Yearbook*, it tells you to send three chapters and a synopsis. How can I write a synopsis when I'm only half way through the book. At this stage, I don't know how it's going to work out, how it's going to end.'

Sally Menzies piped up then. 'Och, just make a guess at how it could work out. Each of us can come up with a suggestion. Then you can cobble them all together. It's worth a try. Think of the excitement if a publisher accepted it.'

'I could faint with excitement at the mere thought.'

'OK. Let's do that. We all want to come to your book launch party, remember.'

One of the others said, 'I've got a gut feeling, Paul, that at least one of the publishers you submit to is going to make an offer, is going to want to buy and publish it. I mean, it's so good, Paul. It's written with such genuine feeling and authenticity.'

They were now all fired up with enthusiasm and excitement and before the meeting was over, a believable synopsis had been written. One of the members typed it out, with copies, and put each into an envelope, ready for posting the next day.

Paul said, 'Don't forget the stamped addressed envelope in each, in case they're not wanted.'

'OK. OK. And I'll go to the post office first thing tomorrow, get them all posted and get receipts for them as well.'

'It's so good of you. Good of you all. I don't know how to thank you.'

'You'd do the same for us, wouldn't you?'

'Yeah, definitely.'

'There you are then. Now I think a cup of tea is due now. Don't get up. We'll make it. We've brought a packet of biscuits so we're OK.

'Bashir, one of our neighbours, did a whole lot of shopping for us. Everyone's been so kind.'

'Good.'

Over drinking down good, strong cups of tea and crunching happily at biscuits, they all enjoyed planning Paul's celebration party.

By the time their writer friends left, Clive and Paul felt so much happier and better. They could have danced around the room. Clive said,

'No more poetry, Paul. Every minute of your time now, every ounce of your energy, must be spent finishing your novel. If they accept the first three chapters and the synopsis, they'll want you to send them the whole book right away.'

34

Paul managed to finish his novel. Clive did some of his best painting. Their minds had begun to heal as well as their bodies. They remembered, for instance, that it was the Reverend Denby who had incited the mob to attack them. He had pointed them out.

They even remembered his exact words. 'An abomination in the sight of the Lord. They deserve to suffer. And suffer they must.' And he had pointed at them and shouted, 'There's two of the filthy poofs. Destroy them! Stamp them out! God said man must not lie with man . . .'

They told Jack Kelly about this, plus all the other ways Denby had harassed and persecuted them since they moved into Waterside Way. Jack then had the Reverend Denby arrested.

They wished they knew who the individuals were who made up the mob which so brutally attacked them, but they didn't. Could that mob still be a danger to them, they wondered. Their writer friends thought not, especially now that the Reverend Denby had been arrested and especially with a police officer living just a couple of doors along from them.

Then a great, exciting event happened that chased away every ache and pain, every fear and worry. A publisher wrote to say that he was interested in seeing the finished novel.

The day they received this word, the writers' club was meeting at their home. The members were hardly over the door of number four when Paul yelled to them,

'A publisher wants to see the finished book.'

'Hurrah!' All their writer friends danced around them in excitement and delight. 'Congratulations, Paul.'

'Yeah, but wait a minute.' Paul's energetic delight fizzled out. 'Once I send it to him, he might not like it and accept it.'

'Why not?'

Paul shrugged. 'It's one thing seeing how I've worked it out in the synopsis. He might not like the way I've written it up.'

'Oh, don't be such a pessimist. There's nothing wrong with your writing. He'll love the book. We all love it.'

'You're my best friends.'

'We're readers too. And honest readers. Now, cheer up for God's sake. Smile.'

One of the writers tickled him under his chin and Paul burst out laughing.

'OK. OK.'

'That's the way. As one famous writer told beginners, "Be happy." Be happy, OK?'

Paul wasted no time in getting the finished manuscript away to the publisher. But again, because he had not yet been out on his own, it was his writer friends who packed it up and posted it.

'I've said it before and I'll say it again, Paul. We're really lucky,' Clive said.

'Yeah, I know. In what other profession would everyone be so genuinely delighted at a colleague's success. And tirelessly help them to succeed.'

'Of course, as they've often reminded us, we'd do exactly the same for them.'

'That's certainly true.'

143

'Now, I'll be in agony waiting to get word from the publisher.'

'Let's pray that he'll waste no time in getting back to you.'

That night and the next two nights, as they knelt by their beds as usual saying their prayers, they added, 'And please, Jesus, help the publisher to make up his mind quickly and get back to us quickly to put us out of this agony of suspense.'

35

Bashir thought he'd find out about Gretna Green. He couldn't mention it to Mirza or Sandra without first knowing something about it. They might not even marry people there any more. He hadn't time to visit the place. He had good, hardworking and willing assistants in the grocery but he didn't like to take advantage of them. He decided to go to his nearest library and have a chat with the librarians. He had always found librarians kind and helpful and he had visited a great many Glasgow libraries over the years. He had friends in every one of them and he always enjoyed a chat. People were his thing. He loved all sorts of people. None more so than Mirza and Sandra.

He'd done his best to help Mirza and Sandra by talking to Pop and trying to persuade him to see Mirza and Sandra's point of view. Sadly it hadn't worked. One of the alternatives was this idea about Gretna Green.

It turned out that there were indeed still marriage ceremonies performed there.

Gretna Green was a village in the south of Scotland, famous for runaway weddings. It was historically the first village in Scotland following the old coaching route from London to Edinburgh. One librarian friend told him that the Quintinshill rail crash happened near Gretna Green, with 227 deaths, making it the worst rail crash in Britain. A troop train taking troops of the Royal Scots to fight in Gallipoli ran into a stationary local train. Then the wreckage of the two trains was hit by a northbound express. This saddened Bashir.

Then his attention was caught up with the fact that Gretna's famous runaway marriages started because of Lord Hardwicke's Marriage Act in 1753 which said that both parties to a marriage had to be at least twenty-one years old. The Act didn't apply in Scotland where it was possible for boys to get married at fourteen and girls at twelve years old with or without parental consent.

Many elopers fled England and the first Scottish village they came to was Gretna Green. The local blacksmith, as the most respected tradesman in the community, became know as an 'anvil priest'. Gretna Green was still the most popular wedding venue and now thousands of couples from all over the world came to be married 'over the anvil' at Gretna Green.

The World Famous Old Blacksmith's Shop, also called the Old Smithy, was the best-known venue. It now had three wedding rooms, each with an anvil.

Gretna was built from scratch as a township during the First World War. It housed workers from the massive munitions factories developed in the area. Bashir thought it amazing that from something so destructive could become a happy and loving wedding centre.

Gretna originally had the largest munitions factory in the world. A workforce of thirty-thousand people produced vast quantities of cordite, or devil's porridge. Bashir shuddered at the idea. God alone knew how many people had been killed by this devil's porridge.

The first chance he got, he spoke to Clive and Paul about marriages at Gretna Green.

Paul said, 'When are you going to tell Mirza?'

Bashir hesitated worriedly. 'I was wondering if it would be either wise or safe to say anything to him just now. Maybe I'd better wait until Pop and Rasheeda leave for Pakistan. As you said, Clive, Mirza and Sandra would want to dash off to Gretna Green immediately and Pop would go after them or get someone to go after them and bring them back before they reached Gretna Green.'

'Yeah,' Paul nodded. 'Safest to keep quiet just now. Wait until the old man's well on his way, or has already arrived in Pakistan.'

'And then . . .' Bashir's brown face lit up. 'What joy! Just think how delighted and excited Mirza and Sandra will be. I'll go with them and see them safely hitched.'

'We could go as well. Make a real party of it,' Clive said. 'Couldn't we, Paul?'

'Yeah. Better watch though. In case they do something rash on their own. No way is Mirza going to risk hanging around while the old man gets a Pakistani bride for him.'

'I never thought of that.' Bashir looked worried again. 'God, what should I do for the best.'

'Maybe you could drop hints. You know, tell him there's no need to worry. You've found a way to help him and Sandra. Or "Don't worry. You and Sandra are going to be married. I've arranged it." Something like that.'

'OK, I'll try that. It would be terrible if they ran away just now, or did something reckless. It would spoil everything.'

The first chance he got, Bashir spoke to Mirza. He had seen him kiss Sandra in the front garden and prayed that no one else had seen them. Jack and Mae Kelly must have, because Mae was out at her front door greeting Jack on his return from work. But the Kellys were all right about the young people. It turned out though that Mrs Jean Gardner did see them and came rushing out to tut at Sandra and advise her to get back into her own house at once, and she was going to report her to her mother.

'I feel it is my duty, dear, to tell your mother about this. It'll mean you'll be grounded for a long time, dear.'

And to everyone's shocked surprise (and it had to be admitted – delight), Jack Kelly said, 'I tell you what, Mrs Gardner, I won't say anything about you having spent some time in Corntonvale Women's Prison for embezzlement if you don't say anything about Sandra to her mother.'

Mrs Gardner turned a sickly shade of grey and hastily retreated back into her house.

The others laughed and Mirza said, 'Was that true?'

'Of course,' Jack said. 'One of my pals took her in the police van to Corntonvale.'

Mae Kelly said, 'You never told me that.'

'As you know, I never gossip about my work or my colleagues, Mae.'

They suspected this was not the Gospel truth, but everyone was too intrigued and happy to bother.

'Anyway,' Bashir said to Mirza and Sandra, 'the pair of you are OK now.'

'Thanks, Mr Kelly,' Mirza said and Sandra echoed his words.

'No problem. Always ready and willing to help.'

At least that was the Gospel truth, Bashir thought. Both Jack and Mae were a real asset to the place, both always ready and willing to help. What would Doris McIvor do without Mae's help and support, for instance? He suspected poor Doris would have gone completely off her head by now. They hadn't a bit of prejudice against Clive and Paul either. They had always been good supportive friends to them.

The Kellys gave them all a wave and Jack disappeared into house number one, Mae into house number two.

Then Mirza said, 'Yes, that's us OK now. But for how long? Any time now, my dad's going to Pakistan to bring back a

148

woman to marry me off to. Or that's what he thinks. But no way am I just going to wait here for that to happen.'

'Nor me,' Sandra said. 'We're off, the pair of us. Aren't we, Mirza?'

'Definitely.'

Bashir put a finger to his lips. 'No need. I've got a plan. Trust me. You and Sandra are going to be married. I've got it all arranged.'

Then he winked at them.

36

Mahmood made Mirza stand before him. 'Do not worry, my son. You are a clever boy and a tall, handsome boy. I will have no difficulty finding you a wife. Do you trust me to do my best for you?'

'Yes, father,' Mirza replied with lowered eyes.

'Your mother is coming with me and she will help and advise me because she too wants to do her best for you. Do you believe that to be true, Mirza?'

'Yes, father.'

Once they'd returned home after seeing his father and mother off at the airport, Mirza said to Bashir, 'I hate deceiving my father and mother.'

Bashir said sadly, 'What choice do you have?'

'If only I could have persuaded him to accept Sandra.'

'I tried, Mirza. I really did try but it only made him decide to go to Pakistan even sooner than he'd originally intended.'

'I know. Thanks for trying anyway, Bashir.'

'Now, cheer up. Didn't I promise you that you're going to marry Sandra? Didn't I tell you that you'd be safely married to her before Pop gets back?'

'Yes, and I trust you, Bashir. But now I want to know how you're going to manage it.'

'Have you never heard of Gretna Green?'

Mirza hesitated. 'The name vaguely rings a bell.'

'You're probably too young to know about it, but it's a village just across the border from England and for centuries, it has married runaway couples. In England couples had to be twenty-one to be married. In Scotland anyone of sixteen years of age can be married without their parents' consent. It used to be even younger. At first it was the local smiddy, or blacksmith, that married couples over his anvil. When we get there, you'll see the white-washed cottage has a sign above it saying, 'This is the World Famous Old Blacksmith's Shop, marriage room.'

Mirza laughed excitedly. 'You mean we could be married there? In Gretna Green?'

'Yes, definitely. But not in the old blacksmith's shop. It's a museum now. But the World Famous Old Blacksmith's Shop now has three wedding rooms, each with an anvil. So you'll still be married in the historic way, over the anvil.'

'When will we go, Bashir?'

'Right now. I've organised everything. You've arranged to meet Sandra, haven't you?'

'Yes, like you said. But wait until she hears you've organised everything. She'll be over the moon.'

At first Sandra was so flabbergasted, she was speechless. Then she jumped up and down, crying out, 'Hurrah, hurrah!'

'For pity's sake, be quiet,' Bashir commanded. 'You'll spoil everything.'

Immediately Sandra put her hand over her mouth and was silent.

'My car's parked round at Jack Kelly's end. He's waiting there with Clive and Paul. Poor Clive and Paul still look the worse for the wear and haven't yet got their strength back but they were determined to come and see that you got a good send off. We've booked rooms at a local hotel.'

151

Sandra smoothed back her cloak of golden red hair and closed her eyes in ecstasy.

'This is all so wonderful. Oh Bashir, God bless you.'

'Aye, well, I don't know if that's likely to happen but I'm willing to take the risk.'

Mae Kelly had done her bit by seeing that Sandra had a pretty dress ready to wear for the occasion.

Now she told Sandra, 'I can't go with you to the ceremony because I can't leave Doris for all that time. But I wish you every happiness, Sandra.'

Then she waved them off, before hurrying back to house number two.

Mirza and Sandra bundled into Bashir's car and soon they were on their way. Jack Kelly followed behind with Clive and Paul in his car.

'There's lots of great stories and fascinating history about Gretna Green,' Bashir told Mirza and Sandra as he drove along. 'At one time, of course, marriages were sealed by both parties holding each other's hands through a hole in a large stone.'

'No!' Mirza laughed.

'Yes. In the Orkneys, it's still known as Odin's Stone. But there's been even odder things happened at Gretna.'

'Why Gretna, I wonder.' Sandra said.

'Well, you see, the law in Scotland hadn't been changed and the first village over the border on the main road from London through Carlisle was Gretna Green. You could get married there right away within five minutes, and without parental consent. No problem.'

'Marvellous,' Sandra said.

'So now,' Bashir went on, 'people come from all over the world to be married at Gretna. There's even a barge on the waterways of Holland called Gretna after the Dutch couple who owned the barge were married there.'

Bashir laughed. 'Even if you didn't have a ring, it was no problem. One anvil priest, as they were called at the time, came up with what looked like a curtain ring.'

Bashir's voice took on a mock solemn note. 'Are you both unmarried persons?'

'Yes!'

'Do you take this woman you hold by the right hand to be your lawful, wedded wife?'

'Yes.'

'Do you take this man to be your lawful, wedded husband?'

'Yes.'

'Before God and these witnesses, I declare you married persons and whom God hath joined, let no man put asunder.'

Mirza raised an incredulous brow.

'Was that all?'

'Yes.'

Sandra said, 'Not very romantic.'

'Och, don't worry,' Bashir assured her. 'Yours will be a lot better than that, believe me.'

And they did.

37

Mahmood and Rasheeda arrived back from Pakistan with a beautiful Pakistani girl. She was modestly and suitably veiled but indoors it became obvious that she was very beautiful indeed.

'There you are, Mirza,' Mahmood announced proudly. 'I have brought you the most beautiful girl in Pakistan. Her name is Parveen. You will be most happy married to her. We will immediately arrange the marriage ceremony and celebrations.'

'That will not be possible, Father,' Mirza said.

'Of course it is possible. Why should it not be possible?'

'Because I am married already. Sandra and I were married while you were in Pakistan.'

Mahmood tottered over to a chair and collapsed down on to it.

'How can that be so? It is not possible.'

'I have a wedding certificate to prove it. I told you, Father, in Scotland it is the law that anyone over sixteen can be married without the consent of their parents. We were married in Gretna Green. It is where runaway marriages take place. Long ago, I told you that I wanted to marry Sandra, Father. Now she is Mrs Shafaatulla, my lawful, wedded wife.' His voice loudened as he called, 'Sandra.'

Sandra entered to stand by his side, her long thick cape of red-gold hair lighting up the room.

Bashir said then, 'And you must admit, Pop, Sandra is exceptionally beautiful. Mirza is a lucky boy, a very lucky boy, to have such a beautiful wife.'

At last, Mahmood found his voice. 'You will leave this house now and for good, Mirza, and take that girl with you. I never want to see either of you again.'

'Och, Pop . . .' Bashir began, but Mahmood interrupted him with a yell of fury.

'You would be the cause of this, you wicked man. You would arrange it all and make it happen. They could not have done it or known how to do it themselves. I would banish you as well if it was not that you are needed to run our business and without a business, we starve.'

'But they have always loved one another, Pop. You've known that all along. Why can't you just be happy for them?'

'And what does her mother say to this? No doubt, the same as me. It is wicked to disobey your parents.'

'Yes, she has disowned Sandra and put her out as well, and I think that's what's wicked, Pop.'

'You shut your wicked mouth and get them out of here. Now, what am I going to do with beautiful Parveen?'

Suddenly Bashir grinned. 'Give her to me in marriage.'

'What?'

'Why not, Pop? I need a wife. You've said so yourself more than once.'

'Yes, but . . .'

'Then we can all live here together as a proper, happy family.'

'Not him and that white Christian girl. That's too much for any devout Muslim father to put up with.'

'Och, all right, they can stay with Mae Kelly at number two until they move into their own place tomorrow.'

'Their own place?' Mahmood echoed incredulously.

'I'm helping them, Pop, financially as well as in every other way.'

'You are a fool, Bashir, as well as a wicked man.'

Bashir grinned again. 'So that's it all settled? I take this woman, Parveen, as my lawful, wedded wife?'

Mahmood hesitated.

'I suppose there is no alternative now.'

'Good. Don't worry, Parveen. I'll be a kind husband to you.'

Parveen smiled at him, then modestly lowered her gaze.

Bashir led Mirza and Sandra from the house and along to number two.

'It's just as we thought, Mae. Pop has disowned Mirza and put him out. But I've got a flat for them over the other side of the Art Galleries. I've finished the legal negotiations. And we've been getting furniture and furnishings moved in.'

'That's great, Bashir.' Mae welcomed them inside. 'You've been so kind to them.'

'And we appreciate it,' Mirza said. 'Don't we, Sandra?'

'Oh yes.' Sandra flung her arms round Bashir's neck. 'What would we have done without you, Bashir? We both love you dearly.'

'Get off,' Bashir laughed. 'If my future wife sees you, she'll be jealous.'

'Future wife?' Mae echoed.

'Yes, I'm going to marry Parveen, the bride Pop brought for Mirza. A real beauty, she is, so I've done all right. I'm happy.'

Mirza said, 'Mae, is it OK if we stay here tonight? The flat will be ready with a bed, etc, tomorrow.'

'Of course.'

Bashir said, 'It's only a one bedroomed flat but it's got a bathroom. The kitchen's small, but there's a good sized sitting room.'

'We love it,' both Mirza and Sandra cried out, 'and it's still near enough the Art Galleries for us to visit there as often as we like.'

Mae said, 'I'm so happy for you. And you'll be especially happy in your own we place, I'm sure.'

Bashir managed to leave despite both Mirza and Sandra hugging him and clinging to him and repeating their heartfelt thanks.

Afterwards Mae sat the young couple down beside Doris. She'd already explained to Doris who they were and as much as she could about their situation. Now Doris held their hands and listened eagerly to their latest news, while Mae put the kettle on.

'What beautiful hair you have, Sandra,' Doris said suddenly. 'I've never seen such long hair before in my life.'

One of her hands stroked Sandra's hair. 'It goes right down to your waist.'

'She's a beautiful person,' Mirza said. 'I've always loved her and I always will.'

38

Bashir was a romantic at heart. And despite the fact that there was no need for the kind of courtship that British Christians had, he wanted to show some feelings for his wife-to-be, Parveen. To her obvious shy delight, he recited Burns to her.

O my Luve's like a red, red rose
That's newly sprung in June;
O my luve's like the melodie
That's sweetly play'd in tune.

As fair art thou, my bonnie lass,
So deep in luve am I:
And I will luve thee still, my dear,
Till a' the seas gang dry . . .

Parveen clapped her hands and encouraged him to repeat another very tender Burns poem that was one of his favourites.

Oh wert thou in the cauld blast,
On yonder lea, on yonder lea;
My plaidie to the angry airt,
I'd shelter thee, I'd shelter thee

Or did Misfortune's bitter storms
Around thee blaw, around thee blaw,
Thy bield should be my bosom,
To share it a', to share it a'.

Or were I in the wildest waste,
Sae black and bare, sae black and bare,
The desert were a paradise,
If thou wert there, if thou wert there.

Or were I monarch o' the globe,
Wi' thee to reign, wi' thee to reign;
The brightest jewel in my crown
Wad be my queen, wad be my queen.

He had never seen Parveen without her head covered and he admired her hair which was like black wings. She no longer wore the burkah indoors and in his presence. It was not a very acceptable garment anywhere in Glasgow, with its dark retreat and tiny slits for eyes.

'More,' she said, with a smile and a flutter of lashes. She was an educated girl and could speak good English. Although he sometimes wondered if she properly understood the Scottish tongue – especially that of the poet, Robert Burns.

'OK,' Bashir said. 'Just one more.' And he went on to recite,

The day returns, my bosom burns,
The blissful day we twa did meet!
Tho' winter wild in tempest toil'd,
Ne'er summer sun was half sae sweet.
Than a' the pride that loads the tide,
And crosses o'er the sultry line,
Than kingly robes, than crowns and globes,
Heav'n gave me more – it made thee mine!

While day and night can bring delight,
Or Nature aught of pleasure give,
While joys above my mind can move,
For thee, and thee alone, I live!
When the grim foe of Life below
Comes in between to make us part,
The iron hand that breaks our band,
It breaks my bliss, it breaks my heart!

But neither Bashir nor Parveen's heart was broken because
their marriage went ahead and was a very happy occasion.

39

Before Jack did the shopping, he had to attend Bashir's wedding. Everyone did, and it was a very happy day. After the wedding ceremony, they all trooped off to a huge hall where a caterer had been booked to serve the six hundred guests. Both Bashir and Mahmood had invited every Muslim they'd ever known in the Gorbals – good customers mostly of the grocery business, but many others in the area and beyond. Bashir also invited many non-Muslims. There were tables seating six to twelve people and one long table at one end of the hall where Bashir sat with his bride and the Shafaatulla family.

The exception was Mirza. Mahmood would have banned him not only from the big table, but from anywhere in the hall. Bashir insisted, however, that Mirza and Sandra must at least be allowed to sit at one of the tables in the hall with his other guests.

The meal was vegetarian and the bottles on each table were lemonade, Irn Bru and water. No alcohol was allowed.

Bashir and Parveen could not go on a honeymoon or holiday because of Bashir's business commitments. The grocery had grown into quite a supermarket and, thanks to Bashir's conscientious hard work, was increasingly successful financially.

Parveen didn't seem to mind. She showed nothing but delight and happiness and it was a pleasure to watch her with Bashir. She kept gazing up at him with such adoration and admiration.

'Ah well,' Bashir said after the ceremony, with one of his wide white grins lighting up his brown face, 'that's another good job done.'

Jack Kelly was there with Clive and Paul. He'd given them a lift in his car. He'd offered Mae and Doris a lift but Mae said she feared it would be too much for Doris. Eventually she was persuaded, however, to come for the meal but not wait for the entertainment that was on the programme for after the meal. And so Jack took the four of them in his car.

'I'll get a taxi back,' Mae said. 'I don't want to drag you away and have you miss all the entertainment.'

'I don't mind.'

'But I do, Jack. I'll only come now if you'll agree to that.'

He rolled his eyes. 'All right. All right.'

During the meal, they all chatted happily together. They shared the table with Mirza and Sandra as well as Clive and Paul. She was glad to see that Clive and Paul looked much better and stronger, certainly more confident and cheerful.

When Mae commented on this, Paul said, 'Actually we're suffering awful suspense just now. A publisher wanted to see my finished novel and I'm still waiting to see if he is going to buy it and give me a contract.'

'We're both suffering,' Clive said. 'Our writer friends all tell us that it's nothing unusual. Apparently publishers usually take quite a while. I have to laugh at the story about Robert Burns, although I'm sure it's not typical. His publisher was called Creech and one day, a friends of Burns' saw Burns rushing down the street brandishing a big stick. The friend asked Burns what he was doing. Burns said, "I'm going to batter my money out of that bloody Creech."'

Everybody laughed, but Doris looked confused.

'Who's Robert Burns?'

'A famous Scottish poet. A very emotional kind of man. I don't suppose his publisher was all that bad,' Mae said. 'He wrote "Auld Lang Syne" and it's recited and sung all over the world.'

Sandra said, 'My favourite of his is "Ae Fond Kiss". I think it's the most beautiful love poem ever written.'

'Yes,' Mirza agreed, 'but so sad. I hope it never applies to us. "Ae fond kiss and then we sever, Ae fareweel and then forever!"'

'No, never,' Sandra said. 'We'll always be together. Always. Always.'

'And so will we,' Clive said, patting Paul's hand. 'We've been through a lot together and survived, and we'll go on surviving. And just wait until Paul is a world famous author with a best-selling novel. That'll show everybody.'

Jack laughed as he poured glasses of Irn Bru for everybody. 'One thing's for certain, we won't get drunk on this.'

'Och, we like it, don't we, Paul? We seldom bother with alcohol.'

'It's a good Scottish drink. If I remember, it used to be advertised as "made in Scotland frae girders" – something like that.'

Doris suddenly said, 'What beautiful red gold hair you have. I've seen it before somewhere.'

Clive said, 'You've seen Sandra often before, Doris.'

'No,' Mae said. 'I think she means the painting in the Art Galleries. We saw it when we were last there. The woman in the painting had a long cape of hair just like Sandra's.'

'That's right,' Mirza cried out. 'I've seen that one. It's gorgeous. Just like Sandra.'

163

Mae suddenly felt sad. The couples at the table were obviously so much in love and so happy. She had once felt like that. She wished she could feel like that again.

Despite this, she enjoyed the meal and before the entertainment was due to begin, she went to the top table, explained to Bashir why she had to leave and wished him and his beautiful bride every happiness.

There was a taxi rank outside and she helped Doris into the first available taxi.

'Did you enjoy the wedding, Doris?'

'Oh yes, it was lovely. Was I ever married, Mae?'

'No, dear. You looked after your mother for many years. It was a strain on you but you were a good, loyal, loving daughter. That's what you must remember.'

'I've got you now, haven't I?'

'Yes, you'll always have me.'

'But you have a husband, haven't you? Wasn't he that handsome man sitting next to you tonight?'

'Yes.'

'He's such a handsome man.'

'Yes,' Mae sighed, 'indeed he is.'

40

'Hurrah!' Paul shouted over the telephone to the president of the writers' club. 'I've had a letter of acceptance. The publisher wants to publish my novel.'

'I'll get in touch with the others and we'll be over right away.'

'I wish I'd known at Bashir's wedding,' Paul said. 'I could have announced the good news there.'

'Don't be daft,' Clive said. 'That was Bashir's celebration day, not yours.'

The writers wasted no time in arriving at Waterside Way and once inside the house, there were joyous hugs and congratulations.

Paul cried out delight, 'I'll be a writer. A real writer.'

'You *are* a real writer,' his friends assured him. And always have been.' They all danced around the room, unable to contain their happiness.

Right away they organised a party – writers only – because as Paul now agreed, only writers and people wanting to become writers could fully understand the sense of achievement and joy a book acceptance brought.

It was an unforgettable night. Alcohol flowed for anyone who wanted it. Everyone came with something – a bottle of red or white wine or a bottle of non-alcoholic wine. Sandwiches and biscuits and cakes were also brought along. Everything was set out on a table in the dining room and on a tea trolley.

They had quizzes and all sorts of literary games and everyone had a good laugh, as well as a good meal. Exhaustion ended the evening at a very late hour. Congratulations were repeated and goodbyes said.

Before going to bed, Paul and Clive knelt down as they always did, clasped their hands and said their prayers, ending with the Lord's prayer.

Then Paul said, 'And thank you, Jesus, for helping me to get my book accepted. Thank you so much for all my blessings . . .'

Next day, they could hardly wait to rush along to tell first of all Jack Kelly, then Mae and Doris, and then the Shafaatullas next door. Because Bashir was needed in the business, he could not get away on honeymoon or holiday after his wedding. And so he was working every day as usual. He was delighted for Paul.

'I'll be your first customer for an autographed copy, Paul. I bet the booksellers in town will have you sitting at a table with a big queue of customers waiting for you to autograph piles of your book.'

'I can just see that,' Clive said. 'Oh, it'll be great, Paul. You're going to be famous.'

'Hang on,' Paul countered. 'It might not sell well at all.'

'There you go again,' Clive said. 'You keep losing confidence in yourself, Paul. You must stop yourself doing that. Think what's happened – a publisher thought so highly of your book he's paying a lot of money for it. You're going to be rich, Paul.'

'Lucky devil,' Bashir said.

'No,' Clive corrected. 'Not luck, talent, Bashir.'

'Yes, you're a very talented guy, Paul. By the way, we haven't seen each other since the wedding but did you enjoy it?'

'Yeah,' Paul laughed. 'Especially the entertainment.' He started singing Indian-type music, flinging his arms up and swinging his body about in an effort to imitate the shapely women dancers.

'It was a really good night,' Clive agreed. 'And what a beautiful wife you have. Where is she this morning?'

'Through in the kitchen with Rasheeda. I've already said goodbye to her. I was on my way out to work when you came to the door just now.'

'We'd better go but we just wanted everyone to know Paul's good news.'

'Congratulations, pal. Your success is well deserved. And lots more books to come, I'll bet. You're not going to be a one-book-wonder.'

'I suppose not,' Paul said, somewhat worriedly.

'Of course not,' Clive said. 'He's full of ideas for other books. He's a writer. Always has been and always will be.'

'Yeah.' Paul brightened and sounded more confident. 'Yeah, you're right.'

41

Mirza and Sandra decided to try the night tour round the Art Galleries. They discovered that when the lights went down at night, it was a different place altogether. Shadows loomed, footsteps echoed round the empty marble halls and exhibits took on a life of their own. In the dim light, the knight on his armoured horse looked as if he was about to leap off his stand in a clatter of hooves and clashing steel. The Egyptian room, which was all about life and death, was especially creepy and it was easy to imagine that the lid of the sarcophagus was about to swing open and release the spirit of its ancient occupant – Pa-ba-sa.

Sandra clung tightly to Mirza.

'It's even creepier than I thought it would be. Especially in this Egyptian room.'

'I know, and there's a really macabre story connected with a sarcophagus. The Duke of Hamilton wanted to be mummified and buried in a sarcophagus. But it turned out to be a woman's one that was sent for him and his legs had to be broken after he died to fit his body into it.'

Sandra shuddered. 'He must have been a right weirdo.'

'He was certainly eccentric. A story I like,' Mirza said, 'is that Dali got a Hollywood stunt man called Russell Sanders to model for his painting of Christ of St John on the Cross.'

'You mean he painted a real person?'

'Yes. He reckoned Sanders had the perfect physique for Christ and had him pulled up on ropes and dangled from the ceiling in his studio while he painted.'

Suddenly Sandra said, 'I love you.'

Mirza laughed. 'Where did that come from all of a sudden?'

'You're so clever, Mirza. No wonder your teachers think you'll do well and get a great degree.'

'So it's just my mind you love?'

She nudged him. 'No. You're very clever in bed as well.'

He turned her towards him and kissed her. Then he smoothed his hands down over her thick curtain of hair.

'You're the most beautiful woman I have ever seen in my life and I adore you.'

The guide cleared his throat to bring everyone's attention back to the tour.

'The Kelvingrove Art Galleries have the only complete set of horse armour in the world,' he said. 'It was made for Sir William Herbert, the Earl of Pembroke. He was one of the most powerful men in England but also a thug and a blood-thirsty murderer.'

Mirza whispered in Sandra's ear, 'So much for our Lords and members of the ruling classes. Give me an ordinary, hard-working man any day.'

'Of course you'll know,' the guide went on, 'that Kelvingrove is full of precious works of art, including paintings by the Glasgow Boys, the Scottish Colourists, Vincent van Gogh, Titian, Picasso, Monet and Rembrandt. These are all best seen during daytime visits. Now, at this late ghostly hour, we have different things to see and experience.'

Mirza and Sandra enjoyed their tour and they were espe-cially happy as, later, they walked back to their new home. They loved their flat and the freedom it gave them. Already, they'd had some of their school friends visiting them. And they'd arranged for Mae Kelly to bring Doris over for a visit. It was good to see how Doris was getting physically stronger. Clinging on to Mae, she was able to take occasional short walks outside. To come to their flat would be her longest walk yet. She still could get confused, repeat things and forget things but everyone knew she was safe enough as long as Mae was along with her.

Mae and Doris were coming for morning coffee and next day, Mirza helped Sandra lay out the cups and the two tiered cake stand which they piled with buttered scones and biscuits. First though, they made the bed together and tidied the bedroom, after which they stood and admired the place and everything in it.

Bashir had been so kind and generous. He'd even allowed them to choose pictures from the Art Galleries gift shop. They had chosen several prints of the Old Masters and the Glasgow Boys and some of them hung in the bedroom. The best were on the sitting room walls for all their visitors to admire.

They'd had lots of visitors so far, mostly their school friends. But Clive Westley and Paul Brownlee had been. Jack Kelly had brought them in his car because, although they were getting better and stronger, they still didn't feel confident enough to walk very far on their own.

When Mae Kelly and Doris McIvor arrived for coffee, they were profuse in their admiration of the flat.

'It's got everything you need,' Mae enthused. 'I'm sure you'll be very happy here.'

'We're already deliriously happy,' Sandra said.

Doris gazed around. 'And you've got it so nice. What pretty cushions and I love the pictures.'

'It's all thanks to Bashir,' Mirza said.

Proudly Sandra poured the coffee. Mirza passed the cake stand around.

'How's Jack, by the way? I know they've been inundated with work at the police station recently. Bashir was telling me.'

'Yes, I believe so, but I'll be seeing him soon. He's anxious to get back to his old routine.'

Mae looked away then, and quickly changed the subject. Mirza wondered if there was something wrong.

42

Jack Kelly fixed a dark stare on Mae.

'There's something wrong here.'

'Where?' Her eyes widened innocently.

'I went to Marks & Spencer.'

'Uh-huh.'

'They had all the steaks and fish and chip suppers that we always used to have.'

'Uh-huh.'

'But it took the whole week's housekeeping money, plus extra money I had on me, to pay for them.'

'Uh-huh.'

'Stop repeating that like an idiot.'

'You're the idiot, Jack.'

'Don't you dare talk to me like that!'

He looked as if he was about to strike her and she said quietly but firmly, 'You'd better not lift a finger to me, Jack. I've already warned you what I'd do. I wouldn't rest until I'd completely ruined you.'

'That's a terrible way to talk. How could you be so malicious, even to think such a thing? You were never like this when I first married you.'

'No, indeed I wasn't, Jack. I've changed a lot. That's because I've suffered a lot.'

'Suffered? What have you suffered?'

'You haven't a clue – even yet. That's how it's always been. You just close your mind to everything and anything you don't want too know about, anything that's too inconvenient to know about.'

'You're raving, woman.'

Mae shrugged. 'Whatever you say, Jack.'

There was silence for a long minute. Eventually, Jack said, 'You haven't answered my question.'

'What question?'

'God, I could kill you, Mae. I'm talking about bloody Marks & Spencer. How was it they charged me so much, but never charged you so much.'

'But they did charge me so much. Any other store would have charged the same. That was the normal price for what you and your pals ate every Sunday. And that's what I had to pay every week.'

'But how could you?'

'I tried to tell you, Jack. I got into debt. You acted the big generous man. You gave me a few paltry pounds that didn't even cover the price of one steak.'

A longer silence followed.

'But you went on . . .' Jack managed at last. 'How . . .?'

'I was scrubbing the floor in the cupboard and I found a loose floorboard.'

'Oh no,' Jack groaned.

'Oh yes. The money I found there solved my immediate problem – the huge bill I was facing for the furniture and furnishings in the house that you seemed to think came free from fairy land. Talk about suffering? Oh, I suffered all right, Jack.'

'Christ!'

'Then there was the torment of trying to save up to replace the money under the floorboards. I managed it, but no thanks to you. I tried, and tried, and tried to tell you and plead for your help, but all you could think of and talk about was the next big juicy steak you were looking forward to enjoying.'

After another silence, Jack said, 'Let me first of all think if there's anything illegal you could be charged with.'

'Good God, you're putting your job first, even now.'

'It's for your sake . . .'

'Oh shut up, Jack. All I want to hear from you now is goodbye.'

'Don't be like that, Mae. We can work this out and start again.'

'You think so?' As usual, her sarcasm was lost on him.

'Yes, I do. And let me start by offering you my sincere apologies for all that I've inadvertently put you through. I'm terribly sorry, Mae. I really am. I don't know how I could have been so stupid.'

She thought selfish was the more appropriate word but managed not to voice it.

He moved nearer to her, making her heart quicken. He had always oozed sex. Other women believed so too.

'My word,' someone had recently remarked, 'that's a real sexy hunk of a husband you've got, you lucky wee devil.'

Jack Kelly was sexy all right. There could be no denying that.

But he was not going to get round her or win her back that way, or any other way. She'd had enough of him. More than enough.

Just then, Doris came downstairs from her bedroom, where she'd been having an afternoon nap.

'Who is that?' She pointed at Jack.

'Jack Kelly,' Mae said. 'My ex-husband.'

174

'Not ex-husband,' Jack said firmly. 'I'm Mae's husband – past, present and future. Now, how about a nice cup of tea?'

'And a nice juicy steak?' Mae said. Jack gave a roar of laughter. He actually laughed.

43

It all turned out just as Clive and Bashir had prophesied.

Here he was, the famous writer Paul Westley, sitting at a table in one of the biggest bookshops in town, signing copies of his novel. As he bent over the books, his long dark hair slid forward, hiding most of his face. He seldom looked up to stare at the long queue of people waiting at the front of the table. Clive, who was standing at his elbow, eventually bent over and whispered,

'For God's sake, Paul. They've been good enough to come. At least look up now and again and give them a welcoming smile.'

Paul immediately looked up to smile, if somewhat shyly, and with some embarrassment, at the crowd of people. Soon he even managed to repeat, 'Thank you for coming.'

When Bashir turned up in the queue, Paul couldn't help laughing.

'For goodness sake, Bashir, I was going to call in at your home with a gift of an autographed copy. You didn't need to come in here and stand in a queue and buy one.'

'I was looking forward to seeing you sitting there just as I'd dreamt and prayed you would.'

'Ah, so that's what got me here.' Paul laughed again and

for the first time, he looked happy and relaxed. 'Muslim prayers.'

'Of course.'

Paul picked up a book from one of the piles and wrote in it,

'To my dearest friend, Bashir, with heartfelt thanks, love and admiration.'

Handing the book to Bashir, he read out what he'd written, then added, 'But no words can convey the extent of my love and admiration for you, Bashir.'

'For pity's sake! You're embarrassing me.'

As Bashir turned to leave, Clive caught his arm. 'That goes for me too, Bashir. To know you is to love you.'

'My God!' Bashir almost ran from the queue but he gave a friendly backward wave as he hurried away.

There had been a photographer present earlier and the photos he had taken appeared in several newspapers. When Paul and Clive arrived back home after the signing, photographers and journalists were waiting in Waterside Way. Paul was forced to stand for a few minutes to have pictures taken before he could escape into the house.

'Did you see that snobby woman watching?' Clive asked. 'I wonder if she'll change her attitude to us now.'

'You never know. Nothing would surprise me any more.'

'Anyway, I don't care if she does or she doesn't.'

'Nor do I. We found out who our real friends are long ago.'

'Bashir's the best one, of course, but Jack and Mae Kelly are close runners up. It's been a help, Jack being a police officer as well.'

'By the way, if that snobby woman suddenly approaches us, trying to be friendly, I'd freeze her out, wouldn't you? She could never be a true friend. Talking of Jack and Mae Kelly, is everything all right between them, do you think?'

'You mean because she's working and sleeping at Doris McIvor's place?'

'Yeah. Seems strange, that.'

'But he goes in there every day. I've seen him.'

Paul shrugged. 'Seems to me a strange set up but I suppose if they're all right with it . . .'

'I wonder how Bashir's getting on with his new wife.'

'You've seen her. She's gorgeous. He'll be getting on great with her. Seems a nice girl too. How about if we slip next door just now with a special signed copy for Mahmood?'

'Good idea. I can't settle after all that excitement.'

'How do you think I feel?'

'You'd better get used to it, Paul. Already there are plans in place for you to travel all over the country doing signing sessions.'

'Yeah. I'm getting worried I'll never have enough free time to write another book. However, I've kept my hand in with doing something creative. I've written a poem and before you object, Clive, it's a good one.'

'I know it'll be a good one, Paul. That's just because you're a good writer. But somehow, in the not too distant future, you must find enough time to write another book. Meantime, read me your poem.'

Paul unfolded the sheet of paper he'd produced from his jacket pocket and began to read:

Conference Dinner

At the long table we sat
seven women and me, strangers linked
by the attentions we pay to words.

Talk began its stream with the weather
meandering into food
then pooled at 'Men'.

Sluice gates opened with a rush
'the dirty, lying, lazy
bastards – present company excepted
of course.' Seven pairs of teeth
gleamed in shared mirth
'Of course,' my smile unforced.

Seven pairs of feet were exposed
skirts and trousers lifted
as the women waded into conversation.
It was as if a tide of oestrus
flowed in concert around me.
. . . bereavement . . . breast cancer
. . . how silly a penis looked . . .
seven pairs of eyebrows raised.
'Present company agrees,' I said.

Now completely immersed
hair waving weightless
around each head like a halo of kelp
conversation was in spate
. . . childbirth . . . work . . . adoption

rather than imposing their own story
on what they heard
or wearing a listening mask
while composing a reply,
the women used both ears.

I would have paddled knee deep
and offered a solution
welcome as a leaking oil tanker
in a crystalline sea.

Afloat on a raft
dry of their experience
I was invited by dint
of gesture and smile
to lean forward, rest my chin
on hairy forearms
to listen and learn.

Clive laughed. 'I like that. I really do. But that's enough poetry now, do you hear me? From now on, you must focus only on novel writing. These signing sessions will finish eventually. Then you must sit down full time to write another novel. OK?'

Paul said, 'OK.'

'Promise. On your honour.'

'Yeah, yeah,' Paul laughed. 'You're a hard taskmaster, Clive, but I promise – no more poetry.'

44

'Look,' Jack Kelly said to Mae, 'I'll drive you and Doris to the Art Galleries and that means she'll have more energy left to walk around and see the exhibits.'

'All right. All right,' Mae said, just to get a bit of peace. She was seeing more of him now and getting more attention from him now than she'd ever done in the past.

Happily he went to get the Mini and once it was parked on Waterside Way, he came in to take Doris's arm and her arm and lead them both outside.

Mae and Doris sat in the back seats of the car and Doris whispered to Mae, 'He's so handsome, isn't he. But he limps. It is arthritis?'

'No, an injury he got at the Ibrox football disaster.'

'Oh dear, poor man. He's so handsome, isn't he?'

Mae thought, 'If she says that again, I'll scream.' She was beginning to realise the true lasting effects of the stress Doris had gone through with her mother's condition. Although Doris was very much better and in fact really quite able to be on her own, she still suffered from occasional bouts of repetition and forgetfulness.

They had a cup of tea in the Art Galleries' café and then

a look round the gift shop. After a rest and another reviving drink of tea, they went to view the Italian art display. Jack kept putting his arm around Mae's waist and she had to keep pushing him off – not because it was unpleasant, but because it was too pleasant.

Doris said, 'Isn't that lovely?' And she read aloud, '*Madonna and Child with Angels* – Tempera and gold on a wooden panel.'

Doris particularly liked *The Annunciation* by Sandro Botticelli. It was a wonderfully realistic depiction of three-dimensional space where the Angel Gabriel hurries to tell the Virgin Mary that she is to bear God's son, Jesus. Doris admired too Bellini's *Madonna and Child* but by the time they reached Titian's *The Adulteress brought before Christ*, Mae was exhausted, although more with the strength of her emotions rather than physical fatigue.

'It's time we went back home, Doris.'

Jack could be a selfish, thoughtless fool, almost to a comical degree at times, but damn it all, despite the anger, the fury at times, he'd aroused in her, she still loved him with all the passion she'd always felt for him. Despite all his faults, he was such a lovable man. And he had plenty of good points. He was honest, courageous, kindly, friendly and well-meaning. Everybody loved him. Why shouldn't she? After all, as she'd already decided, she had been thoughtless and foolish. She couldn't put all the blame on Jack. Another thing, despite the constant agony the poor soul suffered, he managed to keep cheerful and eager to go out of his way to help friends and neighbours.

Suddenly, she didn't just love Jack Kelly; she was proud of him.

Then, as they were making for the outside, Mae noticed that Jack was using the public phone in the foyer.

As soon as he caught up with them, he said to Mae, 'I've

phoned our neighbours and invited them round for drinks at our place.'

It was so typical of him. He'd never think of saying, 'Is it all right if I phone our neighbours . . .'

What could she do now but go along with the idea? Everyone else would be there and Doris was particularly keen. Everyone, including Jack, seemed to have forgotten that she hadn't lived in Jack's house for quite a while.

Once in her old house at number one, Mae helped lay out the glasses and plates of nibbles and crisps.

'It's just like old times,' Jack said, and put both arms around her waist.

She sighed. 'Jack, are you going to behave yourself in future?'

He grinned at her. 'You mean – no sex?'

'You know fine that's not what I mean. You'll have to face facts, especially about the cost of everything. Especially the cost of feeding half the police force every Sunday.'

Jack's handsome face turned serious.

'Oh God, Mae, I can't bear to think of how I must have made you suffer. I'm so sorry for being so blind and so bloody selfish. But rest assured that we'll face everything together from now on. We'll discuss everything and work everything out in a sensible and practical way. But I need you, Mae. Can you ever forgive me?'

'There's only one way I can forgive you, Jack.'

'What's that?' Jack asked anxiously.

'If I can go on loving you the same as I've always done.'

'Oh Mae.' He gathered her up in his arms. Then he let her go and lifted a glass of wine from the nearest table.

'Lift your glasses, everybody,' he called out to the gathering of friends and neighbours, all happily chatting to each other and crunching on crisps, 'and drink to love and marriage and everlasting happiness.'

Mae lifted her glass too and smiled at Jack.

'To love and marriage and everlasting happiness.'

And everyone gave a resounding cheer of joy that hit the rafters.